CAFFEINE
BEFORE CURSES

LATTES AND LEVITATION - BOOK 1

CHRISTINE POPE

Dark Valentine Press

CHAPTER 1

All the Buzz

Deanne Daniels, my best friend and Levitation Latte's one and only employee, came into the coffee shop that morning with a glint in her bright blue eyes that told me something was up. I knew this because no one should look so perky at six o'clock in the morning, especially since I knew she waited to have her first cup of coffee until she got to work, where the brew I provided, with its beans roasted and ground in-house, was vastly superior to anything she might whip up at home.

Following our usual ritual, I got out a cup and poured her some of the Italian roast I'd just made. Unadorned black, because, despite her cheerful blonde looks—the direct opposite of my own dark eyes and hair, traits I'd inherited from my Italian mother—Deanne didn't have any use for the more frou-frou drinks the shop offered and preferred to get her caffeine straight up.

She took the cup, inhaled its aroma, and said after taking an approving sip, "You'll never guess."

"Guess what?" I responded, doing my best not to sound too suspicious. Because I came in about forty-five minutes earlier than Deanne so I could get each morning's batch of muffins and pastries going, I'd already had my own caffeine fix—that particular Wednesday, a cappuccino with freshly grated cinnamon sprinkled on top, a beverage not as nearly high-octane as the one my friend was currently consuming. Even so, I felt a little off, a little jangly. I couldn't say why exactly, except I'd learned over the years to trust my instincts when they tried to tell me something out of the ordinary was looming on the horizon, like the approaching clouds of a summer monsoon.

My Grandma Maureen had told me it was the Sight, that I'd inherited that strange psychic power from her own mother, who'd come to the United States from Ireland in the early 1920s and who apparently had brought her own superstitions with her. When I first started having strange dreams and odd feelings about people or places right around the time I turned thirteen, I'd thought it was just another embarrassing byproduct of going through puberty, like the breakouts on my chin or the way I had to start wearing a bra around the same time. But no, my grandmother said my dreams and weird little twinges and bursts of inspiration were much more than that, and even though the strange gift had apparently skipped a couple of generations, it had decided to manifest itself in me, for whatever reason.

Over the intervening fifteen years, I'd mostly learned how to deal with my quirky talents. Or rather, while most of the locals here in Las Vegas knew there was something a little off about Skye O'Malley, they still accepted me as one of their own.

Yes, Las Vegas. Not Sin City, but "Little Las Vegas," a town in northern New Mexico that, to most people, wasn't much more than a place to stop for gas and a bite to eat on their way to Denver as they headed north on I-25. To me, it was my hometown, the only place I'd ever really known.

And a lot of people would probably even recognize the spot where my coffee shop was located, even if they'd never been to Las Vegas, mostly because my small town had been used over the years as the site of many film and television productions, thanks to its Anytown, USA, vibe and its close proximity to the booming movie industry in Albuquerque. In fact, Deanne's husband Mike worked in Las Vegas's community development department as the town's TV and film liaison...a connection I guessed was directly linked to her next words.

"Guess who's going to be coming here at the beginning of September to start filming a movie?" she asked, blue eyes still dancing. She sipped some of her coffee and waited, one corner of her mouth twitching with hidden amusement.

"I have no idea," I replied, which was only the truth. While I tried to pay attention to this kind of news, mostly because a film or television production landing in town usually meant a boost to my bottom line, I'd been busy all summer finalizing the remodel of the house I'd inherited from my grandmother, and I'd been caught up in choosing countertop materials and deciding which walls to knock down. For whatever reason, my Sight or whatever you wanted to call it had apparently deserted me for the moment.

A small silence while Deanne took another sip of coffee, probably to draw out the tension. Then she cracked a smile and said, "Max Sullivan."

I did my best to maintain a neutral expression, even though my heart felt as though it had dropped to roughly the same level as the flats I was wearing... or maybe even the basement beneath my feet. "Oh?" I said, doing my best to sound unaffected by this unwelcome piece of news.

Because Deanne and I had known each other since the third grade, this study in supreme indifference didn't fool her for one second. Still smiling, she said, "Yeah, Max is starring in a new film by Perry Lockhart. They're going to start filming the day after Labor Day. Cool, huh?"

"Sure," I said, even though the name "Perry Lockhart" didn't mean anything to me. The director, I assumed. Deanne tended to stay up on the who's who of Hollywood much more than I did, thanks to her husband's work with the community development department.

Not that I really cared who was directing the movie. No, the news that Max Sullivan was returning to Las Vegas was a much bigger deal.

Max was literally my "boy next door." A year older than I, he'd grown up in the big Craftsman-style house right next to my grandmother's place, and from an early age, I'd had a painfully massive crush on him. To my infinite relief, he never seemed to notice my fixation on him, had always treated me as the little sister he'd never had, with a sort of good-natured friendliness that never went any further than an off-hand geniality. In a way, that was good, just because Max was the popular guy at every school we'd attended, a golden child who seemed to sail through life without a care in the world.

I, on the other hand, the daughter of a woman

who'd disappeared when I was only a baby and whose father had spent the next ten years slowly drinking himself to death, was someone who'd felt as though she could use the protection of someone like Max Sullivan. Thank God he'd provided that protection, mostly because I was someone who'd been around for most of his life and therefore was somewhat shielded by his popularity, even if I never ran with his in-crowd.

All the same, it hurt to love him so unreservedly and know he'd never return those feelings —not Max, who could have anyone in the world and certainly wouldn't want skinny, dark Skye O'Malley. When he went off to college in Albuquerque and then was discovered by a talent agent his sophomore year, launching a meteoric rise to stardom after his very first role in a CW network drama, I'd been happy but relieved. With him safely living his best life in Los Angeles and traveling the world to make his movies, I figured I could put him out of my mind and go on with my own life, doing my best to ignore his face staring at me from movie posters or in TV commercials for his latest release.

Except now it seemed he would be invading my carefully curated existence.

Even as that thought flitted through my mind, though, I told myself not to be so dramatic. I didn't know anything about the particulars of the film that would be shooting here, but just because he was going to be working in the area didn't mean our paths would ever cross. Surely someone as high-profile as Max Sullivan would have an assistant to fetch and carry for him, so I had no reason to believe he'd be getting his own coffee and might wander through Levitation Latte's doors, thereby precipitating an awkward meeting.

Then again, we'd grown up next door to each other. I had to think he'd visit his parents as his shooting schedule allowed, even if he wouldn't be actually staying with them. And if that were the case, he might think coming by to see me would be the neighborly thing to do. He hadn't been back to Las Vegas since he'd moved to L.A. more than eight years ago, had instead flown his parents to see him in Aspen at Christmas, or had rented a house in Maui for Easter. And although Ian and Tina Sullivan tended to be down-to-earth, homey types of people, they certainly weren't going to turn down a bunch of all-expenses-paid five-star vacations, especially if it meant they got to see their son during the holidays.

"You've got a lot churning away in there," Deanne remarked, and I gave a guilty start.

I definitely had been brooding a bit too much.

Since I knew my friend would see right through a shrug, I only replied, "It's just kind of...unexpected."

She tapped a finger against her coffee cup. As

usual, she sported a perfect manicure, this one in a shimmery shell pink. My own nails were longish and pretty enough, but I never bothered to wear any polish, knowing I'd chip even gel nails after only a few hours of burying my hands in pastry dough or fighting with a recalcitrant espresso machine.

"I don't know why you'd think it's 'unexpected,'" she said. "I mean, considering all the movies that film here. Don't you think the odds were in our favor that Max might come back to Las Vegas to shoot a movie someday?"

On the surface, her words sounded like a valid argument. Probably, I'd just hoped that with so many film and TV productions coming and going each year, the odds would still be in my favor that none of them would end up here.

It seemed those odds hadn't been high enough...or maybe my luck had just run out. Either way, I supposed I should be glad I'd never had any desire to go to the "real" Las Vegas and try my hand at gambling there.

"Maybe so," I allowed. At that moment, the oven in the back room beeped, signaling the batch of cranberry muffins I'd put in a half hour earlier was ready.

Saved by the bell.

"I need to get those," I said, and hurried off. As

I went, Deanne arched an eyebrow in my direction, signaling she knew all too well how happy I was to make my escape and avoid any further conversation on the subject of Max Sullivan.

If I knew my friend, though, I guessed she wouldn't let the matter go quite that easily.

To my relief, Deanne seemed to realize I really didn't want to pursue any discussions about Max, or what might happen once he returned to Las Vegas. She was the only person who knew my deep, dark secret, and she obviously could tell I was wrestling with the best way to deal with her revelation about his return to town. Anyway, it was getting close to opening time, and between getting a new batch of muffins in the oven—lemon poppyseed this time—and going down the checklist of everything we had to do to prepare for the morning's onslaught of caffeine fiends, we didn't have much time left over for chitchat.

And okay, not all my customers were caffeine addicts. A lot of them simply liked the ritual of getting a cup of coffee or tea on their way to work, sometimes accompanied by a muffin, sometimes not. When I took over the coffee shop after my grandmother passed away and I had to figure out precisely what I wanted to do with the place, I decided I wouldn't try to be a restaurant, wouldn't offer the range of sandwiches and salads Grandma Maureen had when the place was still called The Tea Spot and it operated more as a general-purpose café. Instead, I put together a batch of ham and cheese croissants every day, and had the fixings to make bagel sandwiches as long as I didn't try to get too fancy, but I didn't want to be all things to all people. It was enough to roast my own coffee and put together my own special tea blends in addition to the usual Darjeeling and Earl Grey and fragrant green tea, offer some yummy munchies to go along with the drinks, and do my best to make Levitation Latte the very best coffee shop in my little corner of the world.

It seemed the news about Max coming to Las Vegas had already spread all over town, because several people asked me about him and the movie he was supposed to be filming when they came in to get their coffee and muffins. Because I knew absolutely nothing other than what Deanne had told me, I was able to deflect most inquiries, and simply say I hadn't heard from him in a long time but that it should be fun to have him back home while the shoot was going on.

Nice and neutral. The people asking those questions—Lucy Margolis, my other next-door neighbor, and Tom Turnbull, who lived across the street—were just being friendly. None of them knew that Max's and my relationship was anything more than that of a couple of kids who'd grown up together and who'd once been friends.

Truthfully, that's all our connection had ever been anyway. Just because I'd wished it could be more—had probably spent way too much time fantasizing about what it would be like to truly be together, to share a home and start a family—didn't change that uncomfortable reality.

And it wasn't as though I'd spent the last ten years pining over Max Sullivan or anything. Las Vegas, New Mexico, wasn't exactly a hotbed of eligible bachelors, but I'd had a few romantic relationships over the years, relationships that hadn't really gone anywhere and yet proved to me I'd done my best to move on and put those daydreams about Max firmly out of my mind. Luckily, the breakups had been amicable enough, or it would have been awkward—to say the least—to be serving those same guys their morning coffee on the way to work.

In fact, one of those exes came into the shop a little after ten that morning. Kyle Isaacs was a deputy with the Las Vegas police department, and such a nice guy that I'd sort of hated to end things with him. Problem was, there hadn't been a single spark between us, a fact that seemed painfully obvious to me almost from the beginning but which he apparently hadn't quite figured out, judging by the way he continued to ask me out in an off-hand manner from time to time, as though he thought if he just kept trying, sooner or later our chemistry would magically sort itself out and I'd realize I was his One True Love.

"Heard the news?" he asked as I poured a venti Italian roast into his trusty go-cup emblazoned with the city logo.

"About Max?" I replied, and Kyle nodded.

"Yeah, they're finalizing the permits now. Sounds like a pretty big deal."

"Do you know how long they're going to be here?" I asked, doing my best to sound casual and as though the answer to that question wouldn't affect me directly at all.

Kyle nodded. He was a decent-looking guy, with medium brown hair and hazel eyes. In high school, he'd played basketball rather than football, as if he'd known his tall, rangy physique wouldn't help him too much on the field. "The permits make it sound as if they plan to be here for three weeks, with an option to extend to four if they need more time."

Somehow, I managed to stifle a groan. Ever since Deanne gave me the news, I'd been hoping that maybe the production would only be here for a week or so, just enough to get some location shots before heading back to Albuquerque or wherever it was they were shooting the interior scenes. The prospect of having Max and the rest of the crew here for nearly a month didn't exactly fill me with joy.

"Oh, wow," I said, since it seemed clear Kyle was waiting for some kind of response to his news. "I had no idea it was going to be such an elaborate shoot." I paused there, wondering if I should ask any further questions or whether I should let it go. Deanne hadn't volunteered any more information about the movie, saying she didn't know much more than what she'd already told me. I knew her husband liked to share what he could with her, but there were security issues involved when it came to spreading too much information about a production that was supposed to be kept under wraps.

Probably, Kyle should have been similarly circumspect about the film's details, but maybe he was trying to impress me...or maybe he knew I wasn't exactly a security risk. What people told me always stayed confidential. That could be why I also had a completely unofficial but flourishing business reading tea leaves for some of the locals, a talent I'd discovered when I was just fifteen and had seen an obvious dollar sign in the leaves left behind in my neighbor Lucy Margolis's cup. I'd told her she should expect some kind of windfall in the near future, and though she'd laughed and said that sounded wonderful but she wasn't going to hold her breath, she became a true believer after she won a chunk of money in the state lottery the very next week. No, it wasn't enough for her to retire to the French Riviera or anything, but even after taxes, she'd had sufficient funds to buy a new car, do the kitchen remodel she'd been putting off for years, and take a trip to Paris with her husband for their thirtieth anniversary.

Word got out, as it does in small towns, and even in high school I saw a few people each week to read tea leaves for them. It was a lot more lucrative than babysitting, that was for sure, although I also watched the neighbors' kids from time to time to supplement my admittedly offbeat income source.

And reading tea leaves also earned me a reputation as the "weird kid," even though Max, bless him, did what he could to make the situation seem perfectly normal, and no weirder than working part-time as a stock clerk at the local Walmart. I had every reason to believe I would have been mercilessly teased for being Las Vegas's resident fortune teller if it hadn't been for his quiet intervention.

Kyle took his go-cup from me and lifted it to his nose so he could inhale the rich aroma wafting from its interior. The coffee was way too hot to drink yet, but he didn't seem to mind, only set it down on the counter so we could continue our talk.

"It sounds like the director wants to do as

much location shooting here as possible," he said. "I guess the movie is some kind of period piece set in the 1930s or something. Anyway, I guess they're going to be here for a while. They're pretty much taking over the Plaza Hotel as their headquarters."

Which made a lot of sense. The Plaza was a historic hotel that had been completely restored top to bottom about ten years earlier, and definitely was the nicest place to stay in Las Vegas. True, it was also supposed to be haunted by a particularly active ghost, and so I wasn't sure whether the cast and crew could really count on getting a decent night's sleep while they were staying there.

I honestly couldn't comment on the presence of the ghost, since I'd never encountered the guy. Yes, I'd gotten a creepy-crawly feeling while wandering around the public hallways on the bottom floor, where the bar and restaurant were located, but maybe that was just because I'd been expecting to see a ghost and then didn't quite know what to do when I hadn't. Ghost or no, being situated right on the town square guaranteed the crew could probably walk to a lot of the locations they planned to use in the downtown area.

On the other hand, the Plaza Hotel was only about a three-minute stroll from my shop. I wasn't sure I liked the idea of Max being quite that close the entire time he'd be here.

"Which reminds me," Kyle went on. "You may have some days when access to your shop is blocked by the film crew, but don't worry—the production company says it's going to reach out directly to all the affected merchants to work out compensation for the inconvenience."

I couldn't quite keep a wry smile off my lips. "What, they're going to pay us off?"

He grinned back at me, showing the half-downturned smile that I'd first thought was so charming but now just looked lopsided. "You make it sound so illicit."

"Oh, I'm sure it's all on the up-and-up," I responded airily. "I just don't know how Cory Bremmer is going to react when a film crew gets between him and his midmorning espresso refueling."

"That could get dangerous," Kyle agreed, expression still amused as he contemplated the prospect of the town's most prominent attorney being denied his caffeine fix. "But I'm sure it'll all get worked out one way or another." The speaker on his shoulder squawked then, reciting some kind of numbered police code, and he shot it a half-irritated glance before lifting his go-cup toward me in a mock salute. "Gotta go. If I hear anything more, I'll let you know."

"Thanks," I said, and meant it. The two of us might not have been dating anymore, but I still appreciated the way he reached out to give me the skinny on what was happening in town.

As I watched him go, however, I had to wonder whether there was any inside information that would be sufficient to prepare me for Max Sullivan's arrival in Las Vegas.

CHAPTER 2

Homecoming King

The gossip about the film crew coming to town didn't die down entirely, but since that fateful day was still a few weeks off, we all settled back into our normal routines. Deanne and Mike celebrated their third wedding anniversary with a blowout party at their house over Labor Day weekend, with what felt like half our graduating class in attendance. In a place as small as Las Vegas, it was sometimes hard to widen your social circle very much beyond the people you'd known in high school.

Naturally, the party guests gossiped about Max coming to town, but since no one had any real information to pass on beyond what I'd already heard from my best friend, I could safely avoid most of those conversations. Kyle, off-duty for the night, used the confidence inspired by three beers to try asking me out, and once again I had to shoot him down in the politest way possible. He was too nice a guy to be outright rude to, but I really wished he'd get the hint.

That was why I escaped from the party as early as I could and headed home. Deanne and Mike had bought a house in a new subdivision on the edge of town, and so there was no question of me walking home the way I could have back when we all lived in the same neighborhood.

As I pulled into my driveway, I noticed a shiny black Bronco parked in front of the Sullivans' house and frowned. I definitely didn't recognize the vehicle; Tina Sullivan drove a white Honda Accord, and her husband Ian had a Chevy Silverado pickup.

The mystery of that brand-spanking-new SUV was cleared up soon enough, though. Almost as soon as I got out of my Subaru Forester and locked it up—my plan was to eventually get the garage cleared out so I could park the car inside, but so far I hadn't made much progress on that particular project—Max Sullivan came down the sidewalk toward me.

Under the soft glow of the street lamps and the nearly full moon overhead, I could see he still had the same megawatt smile I remembered so well, the kind of smile that looked as though it could light up a room...and a couple of city blocks while he was at it. An unwelcome little tingle went through me, even as I found myself very glad that he'd caught me coming home from a party, and so my unruly hair had been tamed into some almost stylish waves, and I wore makeup and a lightweight summer dress with a cheerful red and turquoise floral print.

"Hi, Skye," he called out cheerfully, as though the last time we'd seen one another was only the day before, and not almost a decade ago.

"Hi, Max," I said, hoping I sounded as breezy and natural as he did, even though it felt as though I had about a million butterflies swirling around in my stomach. "I didn't know you were coming to town before the film crew got here."

Because even though shooting was supposed to start on Tuesday, I'd heard through the grapevine that the cast and crew mostly wouldn't be showing up until Sunday and Monday. Why they were leaving it to the last minute, I didn't know. Maybe they didn't want to spend any more time in the boondocks than they absolutely had to.

Max shrugged. "I thought I'd come early and get myself settled. I'm renting Sunset Ridge while I'm here for the shoot."

My eyes widened before I could stop them. Sunset Ridge was a big ranch on the east side of the highway from Las Vegas, set on a low hill that provided spectacular views of the eastern slope of the Sangre de Cristo mountains, views that had given the ranch its name. The place had once been a working ranch, but had since been converted into a luxury vacation space, the kind of facility fancy corporations would rent out for a retreat weekend, that sort of thing. I'd never been inside the house, but I'd seen pictures, and so I knew it had been completely renovated and had all the bells and whistles one might expect from that sort of property—a huge kitchen with top-of-the-line chef's appliances, a swimming pool and spa, tennis courts, a putting green, even a bocce ball court.

How much must it cost to rent a place like that? Twenty grand a week?

Not that Max couldn't afford it. I might not have been keeping track religiously, but even I knew he'd wandered into eight-figure range for his past couple of movie deals. Eighty thousand bucks to rent the ranch for a month would be chump change to someone like him.

I knew I was focusing on the logistics of his stay in Las Vegas because it was easier to do that than to think about how great he looked, how until that moment, I hadn't realized how much I'd missed the sound of his voice or the way his smile seemed to light up a ten-yard radius around him.

"Does the place come with GPS in case you get lost somewhere inside?" I asked, my tone joking, and he flashed me another of those high-powered grins.

"Absolutely." His expression turned almost sober then, and he went on, "I was hoping I'd bump into you, Skye. Do you have time to talk?"

That sounded serious. Then again, we'd been good friends for a pretty big chunk of our lives. Maybe all he wanted to do was catch up.

"Sure," I said. Because I'd bailed out of Deanne and Mike's party early, it wasn't even nine o'clock yet, so I couldn't really use the late hour as an excuse to beg off. "Come on in."

I reached into my purse to get my keys as I mounted the porch steps, Max only a few feet behind me. Although I couldn't really see his face, I had to think he must have smiled again when the third step creaked, just as it always had. Over the past year or so, I'd had a lot of work done to the house, including having it repainted a soft gray with deep blue on the shutters and trim, but I couldn't quite bring myself to fix that one step.

It sounded too much like home.

Cool air greeted us as soon as we entered the house, a welcome relief after the oppressive heat of a late August night. We'd had monsoon storms the past couple of days, but this particular Saturday had been clear, with not a single cloud or drop of rain to soften the hot, dry winds.

"Wow," Max said after he took a quick glance

around the living room. "This isn't anything like I remember."

No, it probably wasn't. When I was growing up here, the house had been decorated with a collection of mismatched antiques and some unfortunate chintz my grandmother had acquired in the '80s and never bothered to get rid of. While I loved the place because it was home, it had also felt dark and crowded and closed in. After Grandma Maureen left me the house and after I'd slowly made my way through the grieving process, I realized it really did need a breath of fresh air and had gone full-on "modern farmhouse" on my newly acquired home, opening up the kitchen and completely redoing everything in soft shades of buttermilk white and gray with soft blue accents.

After all, she'd told me on more than one occasion that I shouldn't cling to the past after she was gone and should make it my own.

"I might have gone a little crazy with the redecorating," I admitted.

Max let himself look around for another moment before his attention returned to me. "It looks great," he said, then added, "And so do you."

In that awkward moment, I was glad I'd only left on a single floor lamp and the iron pendant fixtures over the island in the kitchen. Maybe the lighting was dim enough that he wouldn't be able to see the way I flushed at his off-hand compliment.

Although I definitely favored my mother in looks —at least based on the few photos she left with my dad before she took off—I hadn't inherited her olive complexion, my fair skin making my dark brown eyes and hair stand out that much more.

And I was definitely what my grandmother used to refer to as a "late bloomer." All through high school, I'd been skinny and awkward, barely any curves at all, nose too big for my face, and I'd pretty much resigned myself to ugly duckling-hood for the remainder of my days. The year I turned twenty, though, some kind of magical transformation had taken place, and all those sharp angles and odd proportions had smoothed themselves out. It wasn't that I thought I could compete with any of Max's leading ladies, but at least I didn't feel like I had to walk around with a bag over my head all the time.

Too bad he'd already been long gone to Hollywood by the time I felt truly socially acceptable.

"Thanks," I said, since there really wasn't any other way to respond to his words. Once again, I had to be grateful he'd caught me on a good night and not first thing in the morning, when I was lucky to have the time to put on a coat of mascara and a brush of lip gloss before I ran out the door. Then, since I realized we were both standing sort of self-consciously in the living room, not sure what to do next, I added, "Go ahead and sit down, Max, and I'll get us some iced tea. It's herbal, so you won't have to worry about it keeping you up all night."

He took a seat on one of my new linen-covered couches, one leg casually crossed over the other, heel resting against his knee. For the first time, I realized he was wearing faded jeans and a loose, short-sleeved linen top in a light blue that brought out his tan and the clear sky color of his eyes. Completely casual, even though I guessed the loafers he had on had probably cost more than my sofa.

"Sounds great," he said.

I went into the kitchen and got the pitcher of tea out of the fridge, then added some ice cubes to a couple of tumblers and poured a good measure for both of us. To my infinite relief, my hands didn't shake at all during this procedure.

Maybe I really had gotten over Max Sullivan.

I returned to the living room and handed one of the tumblers to him, saying, "This is something called Blueberry Fields. Lots of antioxidants."

He took the glass from me and eyed the deep purple-blue liquid inside. "This isn't going to turn my teeth purple, is it?"

"Not unless you soak them in it," I said blithely, then went ahead and sat down on the couch opposite his. Even though I'd been doing my best to act casual, I wasn't about to take a seat right next to him. It was easier to be off-hand and breezy when there was a little distance between the two of us. "Don't worry," I added, since he still looked a little skeptical. "The last thing I want is your dentist chasing after me."

"More like my director," Max replied with another of those movie-marquee smiles. "I doubt he'd be too happy to have his star show up for the first day of shooting with purple teeth."

No, probably not. "A real stickler for detail, right?"

Max's smile faded. "You have no idea." He paused there and took a sip of tea. An approving light entered his eyes. "That's really good. One of yours, right?"

I nodded. "I make all my own herbal teas. The other stuff—the Darjeeling and Earl Grey or whatever—I get from a vendor."

"That's really amazing, though," he said, and sipped some more of his tea. "It seems like you've found your niche."

About all I could do was give a deprecating shrug. "Well, some might say it was sort of foreordained—the family business, you know."

His expression grew somber. "I'm really sorry about your grandmother."

I wrapped my hands around the tumbler I held, the smooth surface cool against my skin. By this point—my grandmother had died not quite two years earlier—the pain was far enough in the past that I could look at it in an almost detached way, even though I still missed the woman who'd been the rock of my childhood more than I wanted to admit to myself. Most of the time, I was okay with playing grown-up, even though there were plenty of days when I felt sure someone was going to come along and accuse me of being an utter fraud at adulting.

"It's okay," I said softly. "I mean, it's never completely okay to lose someone, but...it could have been so much worse. At least she didn't have to spend the last part of her life in a hospital, hooked up to machines. She went out doing what she loved."

And those words weren't an exaggeration. My grandmother had been active and healthy until the day she died. She'd been hurrying into the kitchen to pull a sheet of cookies out of the oven when the aneurysm struck, and the paramedics told me she'd probably been dead before she even hit the floor. Since it had been a Sunday, we were both home at the time, and the beeping of the timer on the stove was what alerted me that something was wrong.

Well, that and the scent of burned chocolate chip cookies drifting upstairs, where I'd been lying on my bed, reading a book.

My grandmother had never burned a cookie in her life.

And I never could bring myself to finish that book.

"Still." Max stared down into his glass of blueberry iced tea, expression uncharacteristically solemn.

At least, solemn in real life. I'd seen that look on his face in the movies plenty of times, usually right before his character was about to defuse a bomb or something.

"I wanted to come here for the funeral," he went on. "But Jerry—my agent—told me it was better to stay away."

For a second or two, I could only blink at Max, understandably confused by his remark. Coming home for the funeral of a childhood mentor was usually the sort of thing that would read well with the public...or so I supposed. I had to admit I wasn't exactly an expert on public opinion polls and audience metrics, or whatever it was that entertainment types used to gauge the popularity of a given celebrity.

Obviously noting my bewilderment, he said, "Um...I was having some problems with Raylene at the time."

Once again, I just stared at him, not sure where he was going with this. Raylene Brown was Max's girlfriend their junior and senior years of high school, and she'd been absolutely nuts about him. They'd actually tried to maintain a long-distance relationship after he headed off to school at UNM, but he'd broken it off when he came back to Las Vegas the summer after his freshman year of college. Although she and I weren't exactly friends —to put it mildly—I'd heard through the grapevine that she went absolutely nuts afterward, tearing up all the photos she had of him and announcing to her friends that she never wanted to hear Max Sullivan's name uttered in her presence ever again.

Not too long after that, she started dating Evan Bryant, who'd been our high school's second-string quarterback. They got married two months before her twenty-first birthday, and their first baby came along about eight months later. The next child followed in rapid succession, followed by another one about two years after that, and as far as I knew, Raylene was content with her life. Evan's dad owned the local Ford dealership, and he worked there as the assistant sales manager, so they were doing all right.

Or at least, I assumed they were fine. Raylene and I didn't exactly run in the same circles, so it wasn't as though I had inside information about her finances or her private life.

"What kind of problems?" I asked, since Max was looking kind of sheepish and didn't appear too eager to elaborate on that little tidbit he'd let slip.

He let out a small breath and drank some more

blueberry tea. Although he seemed to be enjoying the taste, I also got the impression he would have been even happier if it had been something with a little more kick.

"She started writing these long letters to me," he said, "telling me how she'd made a horrible mistake in marrying Evan and how she really thought we should try again. She wanted to come to Los Angeles and move in with me, was asking if my house had room for the kids."

This last sentence was uttered in tones of fairly convincing horror. I didn't know whether that was because Max had absolutely no interest in his high school sweetheart, or because she'd threatened to bring her kids along. Not that Max had anything against kids, *per se*—he'd hung out with me when I was babysitting a few times, and was always willing to play catch in the backyard or sit through the umpteenth viewing of *Finding Nemo* with whoever I was watching that particular go-'round — but still, having your ex want to move in with three kids under the age of eight was a lot to expect of anyone.

"Yikes," I said. "Sounds like Raylene was having her midlife crisis early."

Max's mouth twitched. "Something like that. Anyway, because we had a history back in high school, I really tried to let her down easy, tried to tell her I wasn't in a place in my life where I was ready to settle down with anyone and that she should try to patch things up with Evan."

Considering how Max had apparently skipped attending my grandmother's funeral just so he could stay safely out of Raylene's orbit, I had to assume that particular approach hadn't gone over very well. And even though I wasn't sure what to think about his comment about not being ready to settle down yet, I told myself in a way that was a good thing, since he was still obviously single. "But she wouldn't listen, right?"

"Right." He scrubbed a hand through his hair, mussing it in an artfully artless fashion that told me he'd practiced the maneuver in front of the camera plenty of times. "It got so bad that my agent had to threaten to go to a judge and get a restraining order, and that finally made her back off. Still, I turned down a couple of projects that might have been filmed here, just because I wanted to make sure to leave plenty of space between us."

Probably wise. I didn't know what had set Raylene off in the first place, but it did seem like the kind of obsession that called for time and lots of distance between the parties involved. I drank some of my own blueberry iced tea, then asked, "So...what made you change your mind and come to Las Vegas for this particular movie?"

Something about Max's posture seemed to relax slightly, as though he was glad to move the conversation to safer ground. "Well, I've wanted to work with Perry for a while now. He's been nominated, you know."

Max made that comment in tones of such significance that I had to assume he was talking about an Academy Award. Surely nothing else would merit such obvious reverence.

I supposed I could see why a project with an Oscar-nominated director would appeal to him so much. His bread and butter for the past three or four years—once he'd graduated to headliner status —had been action movies with the occasional rom-com thrown in to prove he had some range, but I had to believe that getting to act in a film where he'd have a better chance to prove his dramatic chops was something he would have jumped at... even if it meant coming back to Las Vegas and having to dodge Raylene Bryant's unwanted advances.

"That sounds exciting," I said, which was only the truth.

"I think it will be," Max replied before adding, "even if Perry Lockhart is a world-class ass."

I lifted an eyebrow. "Seriously?"

"Oh, yeah," Max replied with a grin. "Total perfectionist. He's been known to make hardened professionals leave the set in tears. But the Academy loves his work, so my agent told me to grin and bear it, and maybe I'll get a nomination for this one."

All this was delivered in a tone of voice that managed to be blithe and confident at the same time, as if Max knew he only had to be involved in the right project to get one of those golden statues to grace his mantel. For all I knew, that was exactly the case. He might have been involved in a lot of fluff projects—well, fluff projects that involved a lot of blowing things up—but he was also a very good actor and always managed to lend an air of verisimilitude to whatever movie he was in, no matter how ridiculous some of the plots and set pieces might have been.

"That would be pretty awesome," I said.

The smile was back. "Absolutely. And it is kind of nice to be here. I've missed this little town."

His words had the ring of truth, but then again, he was a great actor. I didn't quite see how poky little Las Vegas could have the same appeal as someplace as glamorous as L.A. On the other hand, people tended to want what they didn't have. Maybe he'd been craving a slower pace.

Well, he was definitely going to get that here.

We talked some more, mostly about the things that had changed in town since he left and what had remained the same, and then he told me he needed to get home because he wanted to go over the script that evening before he went to bed. Since filming was going to start on Tuesday, I took the excuse at face value. I walked him out to the porch, told him it had been great to see him, and we both said goodbye.

No promises from him to see me again soon, which I told myself I understood. He was here to work, not hang out.

All the same, I couldn't quite hold back a pang as I watched his Bronco—which I assumed was a rental, since it had New Mexico plates—pull away from the curb and head off into the darkness. As much as I'd told myself over the intervening years that I'd grown up and moved beyond my childhood crush, our meeting tonight had proved pretty much the opposite.

I could recite whatever inner lies I wanted, but the sad truth was that I was just as much in love with Max Sullivan as I'd ever been...and I had absolutely no idea what to do about it.

CHAPTER 3

Sour Milk

The next day, the film crew began showing up. Even though Levitation Latte was closed on Saturdays and Sundays, I couldn't quite help myself from coming in on Sunday afternoon, ostensibly to test a new muffin recipe. Of course, my real reason for being there was to check out the goings-on in the immediate vicinity, since I could have done a baking test at home just as easily, thanks to the commercial-grade oven I'd bought for my remodeled kitchen.

So far, though, it didn't look as if much was happening in our historic little downtown. There was definitely a lot more street and foot traffic than one would normally see on a Sunday, even if it was the Sunday of a holiday weekend. A few people I didn't recognize paused to peer into the coffee shop's front window and walked away, looking disappointed. Most likely, they weren't used to stores and restaurants being closed when they wanted them to be open. I'd never been to Los Angeles, but I had to believe it was the sort of place that operated 24/7.

Not my hometown, though. After I inherited the coffee shop and decided to make some changes, I'd briefly experimented with being closed on Sundays and Mondays so I could keep the store open on Saturdays. However, enough customers complained that they wanted to start the week with something caffeinated from Levitation Latte, and so I'd gone back to being closed on Saturdays instead. Which was fine—I liked the idea of having real weekends, even if I generally didn't do much with them.

However, the above-normal bustle on Bridge Street told me I'd probably have plenty of customers the next day. Since that Monday was a holiday, I could have stayed closed, because a lot of my regulars would have the day off and therefore wouldn't have as much need of a caffeine fix.

I knew my curiosity wouldn't allow me to do such a thing, though. No, I wasn't expecting Max to drop by, since the ranch he was renting was located a good ten minutes outside the town's eastern border, but I guessed I'd get to see some of the film's crew, maybe even a couple of the actors if they felt like exploring. He hadn't told me much about the production beyond his hopes of an Oscar for his performance, and yet I hadn't allowed that to stop me. A quick search of IMDB to look up Perry Lockhart had let me know the movie was going to be called *Perdition Row* and that it was partially based on a true story about Prohibition-era Missouri. None of those particular tidbits sounded terribly exciting to me, but I assumed the film would be full of real-world historical grit, the kind of thing Academy voters generally ate up.

The IMDB entry hadn't included a huge amount of details, probably par for the course for a movie that hadn't even started filming yet, but it did let me know that Max's co-star would be Lauralee Peters, an actor who'd appeared with him in one of his earlier films...and someone with whom it was rumored he'd had an affair while filming that previous movie, although both of the parties involved had vehemently denied those rumors.

Discovering that Lauralee Peters would be here in Las Vegas didn't exactly thrill me, but I told myself that Max's personal life was none of my business. And okay, she was blonde and gorgeous in the same way that Raylene was blonde and gorgeous, and about as far from me in looks as a person could be, but still.

I needed to be a grown-up about all this. My meeting with Max the evening before had delivered the unwelcome news that I hadn't been able to quite put my unholy crush out of its misery yet, but I could deal with that. After all, I'd had plenty of practice.

On Sundays, Deanne and her husband were busy at their church, or I might have called her to discuss the way Max had been all but lying in wait for me as I came home from their anniversary party. I wished I could have ascribed some sort of romantic motivation to his visit, but I knew that wasn't the reason why he'd wanted to talk. No, he'd just needed to make sure I didn't harbor any ill will toward him for not attending my grandmother's funeral.

At the time, I'd felt somewhat abandoned, even though I had plenty of neighbors and friends to help me through the ordeal, but I'd told myself I understood. Max was busy, and his wasn't the sort of work that would allow a person to drop everything to go to a funeral. Although I'd missed having him there, he'd sent gorgeous flowers—apricot roses, Grandma's favorite—and a heartfelt card conveying his sympathies and letting me know that he'd loved my grandmother as much as if she'd been a member of his own family.

I really couldn't have asked for much more than that. Learning that he hadn't come to the funeral because he was avoiding Raylene Bryant, who'd decided to have a midlife meltdown at the ripe old age of twenty-eight, might have been a bit disappointing, but I told myself I understood. Max was a public figure and really couldn't risk attending an event that might have ended in some sort of scene. True, Raylene hadn't even been at the funeral, and yet I had to guess she would have found a way for her path to cross his if she'd learned he was in town.

Whether she planned to ambush him now, I honestly didn't know. He'd told me she'd backed off after being threatened with a restraining order, but maybe his current proximity would be too much to resist.

I reassured myself that film shoots always had security staff hanging around, and if Raylene tried anything, she'd probably get hauled off to cool her heels in one of the Las Vegas jail's holding cells. Having to explain to her husband why she'd ended up there might be the sort of thing she would prefer to avoid, even if she mistakenly believed deep down that she and Max were soulmates who should never have been parted.

Besides, the catty side of me had to observe that Raylene wasn't exactly the All-American beauty she'd been in high school. My grandmother had assured me on more than one occasion that, while it was obvious to everyone I was a late bloomer, I should be glad of the fact.

"Better a late bloomer than an early peaker,"

she'd said, and I had to admit there was some truth to her statement.

Raylene had definitely peaked early. She was one of those girls who'd been all blonde wavy hair and long legs and big boobs in high school, but who now looked ten years older than she should. Maybe that was just the stress of having three kids practically back to back, but I knew plenty of other girls from our high school who'd had children early and still didn't look as though they'd aged as much over the past decade.

And all right, I knew it was shallow and down-right nasty to judge another woman based on her looks, and under ordinary circumstances, I would never have allowed such thoughts to even cross my mind. However, since Raylene had expended a lot of energy in high school calling me "beanpole" or "goblin" when Max was safely out of earshot, I wasn't about to beat myself up for thinking lately she looked like a horse that had been ridden hard and put away wet.

So to speak.

Anyway, there was always the possibility that Raylene wouldn't want to be anywhere near Max when she wasn't looking her best, to put it mildly. I could be worrying about absolutely nothing.

At the same time, though, I had to believe someone who'd write scores of love letters to her high school boyfriend and who'd been ready to walk out on her husband based on unreciprocated feelings for a man who had clearly moved on might not be the most stable person in the world.

Well, whatever was going to happen, was going to happen. Maybe I'd get a psychic flash about what she had planned, but I somehow doubted it. My visions and dreams were pretty much always about the people close to me, and Raylene Bryant definitely couldn't be included in that group.

Max, on the other hand....

Oh, stop it, I admonished myself. *You're not going to dream about Max Sullivan. You haven't had a single vision about him these past ten years, so what makes you think you're going to start now?*

Absolutely nothing, I supposed. It was true he'd disappeared from my dreams as soon as he'd left for Los Angeles, as though that weird part of my brain had realized he was no longer in my orbit, and therefore I didn't need to expend any more mental energy on him.

If only my heart had gotten the memo.

Mouth tight, I headed into the storeroom and started assembling ingredients. I'd come down here to test out my new walnut spice muffins, and damn it, that was what I was going to do.

Even if it killed me.

The muffins didn't kill me, of course. They actually turned out great, which meant I'd add them to the lineup come Monday morning. I had the regulars that I always kept in the rotation—blueberry, carrot, the gorgeous cranberry ones that I sweetened with white grape juice—but I liked to switch other offerings in and out based on the season. Since we'd now moved into September... even though the weather didn't feel like it...I figured it was time to retire my lemon poppyseed muffins and replace them with something that felt a bit more autumnal.

Because I didn't think I'd be super-busy that Monday, I told Deanne to go ahead and take the day off. Labor Day was a federal holiday and that meant her husband Mike wouldn't be working, and it didn't seem fair to make her come into the shop when they could be off enjoying some free time together. She'd protested a bit but had eventually given in.

"I really would like to go to Santa Fe with Mike for the day," she'd said when I called her late Sunday afternoon to let her know she wouldn't have to work the next day. "But I don't want to leave you in the lurch."

"It'll be fine," I assured her. "I actually mixed up a bunch of batter already and put it in the fridge, so I won't have as much to do when I open up tomorrow."

"If you're sure—"

"I'm sure," I said firmly. "Now, go have fun."

It did feel a little strange to walk into the shop on Monday morning and realize I'd be there all by myself until I closed up at three-thirty, but it wasn't the end of the world. Deanne rarely missed a shift, because she was one of those people who never seemed to get sick, and yet I'd worked alone a few times, most notably when she and Mike had gone to Mexico for a week for their honeymoon.

That had been a *very* long week.

But this was only one day, and I knew I'd survive it.

Things did get off to a fairly slow start, which was what I'd figured would happen. True, not everyone got Labor Day off work, but a lot of my regulars were employed by the city or county, or by various businesses around town, and so they weren't up and about early on that holiday morning. A few people trickled in who I thought were probably members of the film crew; I didn't recognize any of them, but they didn't feel like tourists, either. They ordered their lattes and macchiatos and Americanos without fuss and headed back out, a few of them buying muffins as well.

And then *he* walked in.

No, not Max. I'd already guessed he wouldn't have any reason to come into town for coffee, unless he had a burning need to see the changes I'd made in the shop. But since he was going to be filming on my street for the next few weeks, he'd have plenty of opportunity to check out Levitation Latte without making a special trip.

This guy seemed as though he was probably in his late forties or early fifties, his fair hair showing a few glints of silver where the sun came through the store's front window. He had lean, aquiline features and the sort of thin nose that looked as though it was caught in a perpetual sneer.

Or maybe that was just his way of expressing what he thought of my coffee shop. He gave a brief glance around, and his eyes narrowed slightly. At once, I bristled—I'd put a lot of effort into the remodel, and thought the place was the perfect blend...no pun intended...of new and old, with a big comfy couch and love seat covered in soft plum velvet tucked into one corner, and exposed brick on the wall behind the gleaming granite counter. Paintings and framed sketches from local artists adorned the other walls, and plants in baskets added a touch of green in carefully chosen corners and nooks.

All of my decorating endeavors apparently were lost on the newcomer, however. Still wearing an expression that made him look as though he'd smelled something bad, he said, "Do you roast your own beans?"

"Yes," I replied, even as I did my best to keep

my tone neutral and not defensive. It wasn't the first time someone had grilled me about my offerings, but I still found the question insulting. I took pride in serving the very best coffee I possibly could, and I didn't like the guy's insinuation that I'd cut corners somewhere. "And I distill my own water," I added, knowing that comment probably had sounded a little snotty and realizing I didn't care very much. "What can I get for you?"

"Double espresso," he said shortly.

I somehow doubted his disposition would be improved by an infusion of that much caffeine, but of course I didn't say anything other than, "Coming right up."

Glad of the opportunity to turn my back on him, I went over to the Breville Barista machine and got the brew going. Even though I wasn't looking at the guy, I could sense how he lingered at the counter rather than taking a seat at one of the bistro tables located just a few steps away. No, this guy clearly wanted to get his fix and move on, which was just fine by me. I'd done my best to make Levitation Latte a welcoming, friendly place, and I didn't need his negative energy polluting my surroundings for any longer than was absolutely necessary.

However....

"To go?" I asked, since he hadn't specified

whether he actually did intend to stay or whether he planned to drink his espresso somewhere else.

His gaze moved over the coffee shop once more, and his lip curled. "Obviously."

Right then, I wished I had the kind of magical powers that would allow me to cast hexes on people. Not big, horrible ones, of course, but just the sort of stuff that would ruin someone's day—a flat tire, a broken crown...a nastygram from the IRS.

But because what magic I possessed—if you could even really call it magic at all—was confined to reading tea leaves and occasionally having prophetic dreams, I knew there wasn't much I could do to reward the guy for his crappy attitude. Most likely, he was already cursed by having to suffer being himself, and I should just let the universe and karma handle him.

I poured his espresso into the smallest of my go-cups and sealed the lid. "That'll be five-fifty."

Still wearing that slight curl of the lip, he reached into his wallet and handed over one of those fancy black American Express cards. The name on it was Perry Lockhart.

Why didn't that revelation surprise me the slightest bit?

It was almost impossible to keep an evil smile from pulling at my own mouth, but somehow I managed it as I gave the card back to him. "I'm sorry," I said in my sweetest tones, even though inside I was grinning in evil glee. "I don't take American Express. Just Visa or Mastercard...or cash, of course."

His brows drew together in a scowl, but he didn't say anything, only stuffed the black Amex card back in his wallet and then pulled out a five-dollar bill and three quarters. "Keep the change," he said, then picked up his espresso and stalked out.

Although my first impulse was to pick up the quarters and throw them at the door he'd just exited through, I knew that sort of childish behavior wouldn't earn me any points. No, I just scooped up the coins, mouth tight, and put them and the five-dollar bill in the cash register. Probably it was the worst tip I'd ever received, but whatever. He'd succeeded in pissing me off, and that was as far as I'd allow him to get under my skin. Still, I had to hope his experience at Levitation Latte had been negative enough that he wouldn't bother coming back. There was a Starbucks up on 6th Street; he could go there to get his caffeine fix.

Or, more likely, send one of his assistants to get it. In a way, I was sort of surprised he hadn't told a P.A. to get his espresso this morning. Maybe he'd figured since they weren't actually working today, he couldn't really ask someone else to run the errand for him.

That theory didn't ring very true, though. Even our very brief meeting had told me that Perry Lockhart wasn't exactly the sort of person to worry too much about whether he was crossing a line.

It sure looked as though Max hadn't been exaggerating when he'd said his director was kind of an ass, except I thought he was being a bit too generous in that assessment. I would definitely have left out the "kind of" part.

And even though I knew Max was probably getting paid the kind of money a girl like me could only dream of, I still didn't envy him these next few weeks of work. He was going to earn every dollar of that eight-figure salary dealing with Perry Lockhart.

If they didn't kill each other first, of course.

CHAPTER 4

Shooting Blanks

On Tuesday morning at a little past nine, just as I was pulling a new batch of muffins out of the oven and Deanne was getting Cory Sills —the mayor's assistant—her usual mochaccino, a man I'd never seen before came into the coffee shop. He was on the pudgy side and had light brown hair scraped back into a skimpy ponytail, and carried a clipboard.

"Can I help you?" I asked, although I had a feeling I knew why he was here. Anyone who wore that kind of nervous expression had to be working for Perry Lockhart.

"Are you the manager?" the guy responded, even as he sent a quick glance over at Deanne. Since the two of us were the exact same age...well, give or take a few months...he probably was having a hard time figuring out who exactly was in charge at Levitation Latte.

"I'm the owner," I told him. "Skye O'Malley. What can I do for you?"

He didn't exactly relax, but at least he looked a little less nervous. "I'm with the *Perdition Row* crew. We're going to be filming in front of your shop on Thursday and Friday, so I need to have you sign these release forms."

By that point, Deanne had finished her business with Cory, and so she turned toward the stranger, a small frown pulling at her fair brows. "Release forms for what?"

I knew she was playing dumb, because she knew all about what a production might expect of businesses involved in a location shoot...and the sorts of compensation that were usually involved.

He shot her a dubious look, as if he wasn't quite sure why my assistant was asking the questions. As someone who was used to a film shoot's usual chain of command, he was probably startled that she hadn't deferred to me.

In this case, though, I certainly didn't mind. Besides, even though Deanne technically worked for me, ours wasn't exactly what you could call a normal employee/supervisor sort of relationship.

"Um, to allow us to set up in front of your coffee shop during those two days," the man said.

"Blocking the entrance?" she inquired.

"Well, probably." As her eyes narrowed, the guy hurried on, stammering a bit, "We, uh...of course we'll compensate you for any loss of business. We'll pay two thousand a day?"

I had a feeling he hadn't intended for his comment to end on an upward inflection, as though he was asking whether that was okay instead of simply offering a flat rate.

Either way, that was more than double what I usually would have earned over the same period. Deanne's expression didn't shift a bit, though, and I could see why she always cleaned up at poker when she and Mike spent an afternoon gambling at one of the local Native American casinos.

Because it looked as though she wanted to barter—and because I guessed this poor P.A. or minor producer or whoever he was hadn't been authorized to offer anything more than the standard compensation—I figured I'd better cut in.

"Two thousand a day should work," I said. "Let me see the forms."

Looking infinitely relieved, he handed over the clipboard. I scanned the paperwork, but I didn't see any gotchas that immediately leaped out at me. The filming would take place Thursday and Friday, September eighth and ninth, and would occur between the hours of eight in the morning and six in the evening. For each of those days, Levitation Latte would receive two thousand dollars for the disruption the production would cause my business.

I scrounged for a pen next to the cash register, then asked, "What happens if you end up not filming for an entire day?"

"Oh, you'll still get the full per diem," the guy replied, still looking happy that I hadn't said no, and in fact appeared to be completely on board with the plan. "It's only fair, since you would have already let your customers know you wouldn't be open those days."

"Fair enough," I said, and went ahead and signed on the dotted line. They hadn't given me much in the way of advance notice, but I'd put a sign in the front window and let everyone who came in between now and then know they'd have to go elsewhere for their coffee those two days. I gave the man his clipboard, and he tucked it under one arm.

"I'll stop by at the end of the day on Wednesday to bring you a check," he promised.

"Sounds good," I replied. "We close at three-thirty."

He filed that fact away with a nod, and headed out. Once he was gone, Deanne shot me a huge grin.

"Four grand to get a couple of days off?" she said. "What're you going to do with all that money?"

I honestly had no idea. Shove it into the business's savings account and hold it against a rainy day, most likely. While I'd spent a decent chunk of change renovating my house and fixing up the coffee shop, I generally wasn't what most people would think of as a big spender.

More important to me, actually, was the chance to have those two days off work. While I loved the coffee shop and wouldn't have traded it for anything in the world, sometimes it did get a little exhausting, having to be up so early in the morning and knowing that so many people depended on me to get their days started with a jolt of caffeine. Being able to do whatever I wanted with this extra time was like a gift from the universe.

"Sock it away, I guess," I said. "You never know when there might be an unexpected plumbing repair, or whatever."

Deanne's nose crinkled a bit. "And here I thought you were going to run off to Paris or something."

I couldn't help chuckling. "No, probably not. I might go to Santa Fe, though, or up to Taos for the day. Just someplace where I can get a change of scenery."

"That sounds like fun." She paused there, and let out a very small sigh. "And here Mike and I just went to Santa Fe on Monday. I'm not sure what I'm going to do with myself."

Did she think I didn't want her to come along on my little expedition, just because she'd had her own trip to the capital city just a couple of days before? "Well, I was kind of hoping we could have a girls' day out, since Mike is going to be working anyway. Or is that too much Santa Fe in one week?"

"Definitely not," Deanne replied, her expression much more cheerful now. "Which day?"

"Oh, Thursday, probably," I said. "You know how that place gets on the weekends, especially at this time of year when the weather's nice."

"Thursday, then." The door to the shop opened then, and her face lit up with interest, but it was just another one of our regulars, Jesse Lopez, coming in for his ten o'clock grande French roast and a muffin. The disappointment in her eyes was almost comical. Not that Deanne had anything against Jesse, but I could tell she'd been hoping the P.A. or producer or whoever he was might be returning to tell us they actually needed to film in front of the shop for a whole week.

I had to shake my head, just a little. "Hi, Jesse," I said with a smile. "What can I get for you?"

After that exchange, I made up a sign to hang in the coffee shop's window, letting everyone know Levitation Latte would be closed that Thursday and Friday. There was some grumbling, but most people just seemed excited that a place they knew well would be featured so prominently in the film. True, the director and cinematographer would probably work hard to make the storefront look different from the way it did in real life—I had a feeling that the shop's sign, with its woman floating in a lotus position as she held a large cup of coffee in both hands, wasn't exactly period-appropriate for a Depression-era movie—but still.

The whole point of the sign was a little joke that the foam in my coffee drinks was so light, it would make you feel as though you were floating. I'd never been into yoga, and I certainly didn't know how to levitate, but I thought it made a fun logo for the business, one I'd had designed by an old friend of mine from high school, Darren Myles, who'd gotten a degree in graphic design at UNM and then came back to Las Vegas to start his own business.

Anyway, it was sort of a game among us locals to watch movies and shows filmed here and then pick out all the various locations and discuss how they'd been doctored in one way or another so they wouldn't be quite so recognizable.

Deanne and I decided to head out around ten-thirty on Thursday morning, putting us in Santa Fe just in time for lunch. Although I hadn't bothered to set my alarm that morning, I didn't sleep in as much as I would have liked to, with the time just cruising past six o'clock when I woke up and knew my body and brain were ready to start the day.

That was all right, though—I took extra care getting ready for our day out, puttered around the house a little, and then decided I might as well cruise by the shop before I picked up Deanne, just so I could get a glimpse of what was going on and make sure that Tilly, the big black alley cat who was the shop's familiar spirit, had plenty of food and water to get her through my absence.

Tilly was even more of an independent creature than most cats, and although I'd tried to coax her to come home with me and have a much more stable existence than hanging around our little downtown area, she would have none of it. No, she was just fine with showing up on the back stoop when she was hungry, and occasionally deigning to come in through the cat door I'd installed if the weather was particularly nasty, but she'd made it painfully obvious she had no desire to become any more domesticated than that.

Which was fine, I supposed. Tilly had amply

proven that she could take care of herself. All the same, I knew I would be derelict in my duty if I didn't ensure she would be well fed in my absence.

The film crew had blocked off Bridge Street, but that was all right—I had a parking space in back, off the alley. I pulled in, turned off the engine, and went up the back stoop to let myself into the shop's combination kitchen/storeroom.

Everything looked in order, although even from back here, I thought I could hear the sound of someone shouting orders. I couldn't make out the words, however. Was that Perry Lockhart, or did he have an assistant director to handle that kind of thing?

I wasn't about to poke my head through the storeroom door to find out. There probably wasn't much chance that a camera would pick up my movements that far away from the front window of the shop, but better not to take the risk at all.

No, I just rinsed out Tilly's water bowl and refilled it, then poured a heaping pile of dry cat food in the other bowl. That would probably be enough to get her through the weekend, since my store wasn't the only place she frequented. All the same, I planned to come back on Saturday morning and double-check that everything was still intact after the film crew had moved on to another location.

The cat was apparently off doing something

else important today, though, because I didn't see hide nor hair of her. However, I knew she came and went on her own schedule, and so I wasn't too worried about her absence.

I got back in my Subaru and headed down to Deanne's house. Her neighborhood was on the south side of town, and therefore on the way to Santa Fe. And because she was like me and probably had been up since dawn, she was ready and out the door as soon as I pulled into the driveway, wearing a pretty embroidered top, skinny jeans, and cute little flats.

Hmm...maybe I should have made more of an effort when I got dressed this morning. Not that I looked like a complete slob or anything, but I couldn't help contrasting my friend's cheery outfit with my black wrap-style knit shirt, broken-in bootcut jeans, and black leather thongs. Black had been my go-to ever since my senior year of high school, and although I had a few pieces of clothing that actually sported a little color—like the dress I was wearing when Max and I had our little talk on Saturday night—the overwhelming impression you got when you peered into my closet was that I must be in perpetual mourning.

Or maybe from New York.

"How's it going at the shop?" Deanne asked as she fastened her seatbelt, and I sent her a sideways glance.

"Why would you think I'd gone by the shop?"

That disingenuous question only got me a raised eyebrow. "Because I know you," she said simply. "I know you just *had* to take a peek."

"I was feeding Tilly," I said, my tone a little more severe than I'd intended.

"Uh-huh. Did you see anything interesting?"

"Not really." By that point, we'd exited the development where Deanne's home was located and were on I-25 heading south. "I didn't leave the storeroom—I just put out some food and water for the cat. But I could tell the film crew was definitely right in front of the shop, so it's good we shut everything down."

She nodded, then pulled a bottle of water out of her oversized purse and set it in one of the cupholders in the center console. A bottle of my own rested in the other holder; I might have made my living serving people coffee, but once I'd had my one cup in the morning, I was generally good on caffeine for the rest of the day.

"Maybe we should go by the shoot tomorrow and see if we can say hi to Max," she suggested.

That sounded like a terrible idea. Yes, a bunch of people always showed up to looky-loo whenever something was being filmed in Las Vegas, but that didn't mean I wanted to act like a complete fangirl.

"I doubt that would go over too well with Mr. Lockhart," I remarked.

Because I'd already told Deanne all about my run-in with the director of *Perdition Row,* she didn't seem too surprised by my comment. Even so, she shrugged and said, "Well, if other people are watching the shoot, it's not like he can tell us to stay away."

"Maybe not, but I'd rather just wait and watch the finished product," I said. "You know how much the security guys hate having to ride herd on a bunch of gawkers."

"I suppose so." She didn't say anything for a moment, only fiddled with the strap of her purse where it sat in her lap. Then she shifted and looked over at me, her expression much more serious now. "Heard anything else from Max?"

"No," I replied. The silence since his Saturday night visit bothered me more than I wanted to admit, even though I knew he must have been doing some serious prep for his role and probably didn't have any time for hanging out. No, he most likely thought that, since he'd cleared the air with me, we didn't have a whole lot left to say to each other. Our lives were completely different now. Why should I expect him to resume a friendship he'd left behind almost a decade earlier?

"I'm sorry," Deanne said, and I took my eyes off the road long enough to allow myself a quick glance at her face. She seemed awfully serious, clearly troubled...and that was a reaction I definitely didn't want from her. This was supposed to be a fun girls' day out, after all.

"Don't be," I told her. The day after Max's visit, I'd told her about what had happened, and how things were just fine between him and me. Or rather, we were being friendly, which was about all I could ask for. Expecting anything else from someone of his stature was just crazy. "He's really busy. Maybe we'll all be able to get together and have a beer or whatever once filming is done, but he's got other stuff to focus on right now."

"True." Her expression cleared as a faint smile touched her lips—probably as she was imagining a get-together at my place, just a bunch of us regulars hanging out with the one guy from Las Vegas who'd managed to make it big. Maybe such a gathering would always be a fantasy and nothing more, but I wasn't about to burst her bubble.

Not when I'd been entertaining similar thoughts—idle notions about the two of us sitting together on my front porch and having a lemonade as we talked about what we'd been up to these past ten years, or hopping in the car and spending a day together in Santa Fe—foolish as they might have been.

Luckily, Deanne picked up on my vibe, because she didn't say anything else about Max, instead asking me where I wanted to eat lunch. We launched into a lively discussion of the various merits of several downtown restaurants, eventually deciding to go to The Shed, since neither of us had been there recently.

Totally normal, which was exactly what I wanted.

Even so, I couldn't help wondering how the day's shoot was going.

Apparently, it had been an uneventful day back in Las Vegas, because when I swung by the shop that evening after I dropped Deanne off at home, I couldn't spy a single shred of evidence that a film production had even occupied the sidewalk in front of Levitation Latte. In fact, everything looked neater and cleaner than usual, as if they'd made sure to have a couple of crew members sweep the sidewalks and wipe down the windows after they were done.

I doubted Perry Lockhart would be so thoughtful, and guessed the clean-up had been the idea of one of his assistant producers or P.A.s. Either way, I definitely didn't have anything to complain about, so I headed home.

My lunch had been huge, so I didn't bother to make any kind of real dinner beyond throwing together a green salad and pouring myself a glass of ice water. No wine, because I'd had two margaritas with lunch, and hadn't worried about driving afterward because I'd known Deanne and I would wander around downtown for hours before heading home. All the same, drinking in the middle of the day always made me a little tired, and I didn't need any more alcohol. No, I just wanted to put my feet up and watch a little TV or maybe read, and then I could go to bed and put an end cap on my day.

I almost nodded off several times during my mini-binge of *The Great British Bake-Off,* and so I turned off the TV and headed upstairs. All day, my phone had been quiet, beyond a call from one of my suppliers asking to move a coffee bean shipment to the following week. I'd assured him that was fine, since the shop wouldn't even be open again until Monday, and that had been the end of it.

So why had I been hoping for a call from Max?

Because you're an idiot, I told myself as I pulled my hair back for the night in a loose scrunchie. I wasn't much of one for makeup, but I applied moisturizer religiously both morning and night. Earlier that day at The Shed, I'd gotten carded when I ordered my first margarita, and I wanted to keep on getting carded for as long as possible.

Hence, the moisturizer.

It did feel good to climb into my big king-size bed and pull up the quilt. The day had been too warm to crack the windows, and so the central

A/C—another of my recent improvements— hummed away in the background, keeping the room just cool enough that I needed my quilt.

I hadn't really expected to dream. *Dream,* dream, that is. Or at least, the scene I fell into felt like one of my "true" dreams, and not just a jumble of scenes and impressions from the past few days.

Max and I were sitting on the porch swing. Not close enough to one another that the setting felt at all romantic, but there was still a friendly, nostalgic glow to the scene, thanks to the soft, dusky light that fell on the porch and the gentle chirping of crickets in the background. I'd had to get rid of the porch swing of my childhood when I did all the renovations, since it just wasn't safe anymore, but there had never been any question about not replacing it. Having a gorgeous wraparound porch like that without a swing had to be some kind of crime.

When I looked closer, I realized why there was such a gap between the two of us.

Lying on the cushion was a gun.

What I didn't know about guns could fit in a shipping container, but even I could tell it was some kind of revolver, with a shiny nickel finish and elaborate engraving along the barrel. The end of that barrel was pointed away from us, directed out toward the front yard, but its position didn't make me feel any more comfortable about the situation.

Dream-Max must have noted where I was looking, even though my dream-self hadn't moved. He said, "I really don't like working with those things."

"Mr. Action Star doesn't like guns?" my dream-self joked. I could have probably counted on one hand the number of movies he'd appeared in where he hadn't been shooting all kinds of guns—assault rifles, semi-automatic pistols, you name it. Max's father was kind of a gun nut, and so he'd been shooting ever since he was old enough to pick up a BB gun back in grade school.

But the dream-Max's expression was serious as he replied, "I'm okay with guns in the right setting. I just always worry that something's going to go wrong."

"Wrong how?" my dream-self asked. "You take all kinds of safety precautions, right?"

He nodded. "We do. I still worry, though."

And he looked so troubled that my dream-self did something I would never be brave enough to do in real life. I reached over and took his hand, and gave it a gentle squeeze. "It's okay," I told him. "You have nothing to worry about."

His expression lightened just the tiniest bit. "You're sure?"

"Positive."

"Well, then."

He picked up the revolver and hefted it in his hand, as though feeling its weight. "Then I suppose it's okay if I do this."

And he held the gun to his head and pulled the trigger.

CHAPTER 5

Bum's Rush

I sat up in bed, my breath coming in heavy pants. Sweat trickled down my back...cold, thanks to the refrigerated air blasting through the vents in my bedroom.

What the hell was *that?*

It had felt like a true dream...and yet I knew it couldn't be. Max Sullivan had to be the last person on the planet who would ever harm himself. No, the dream probably wasn't meant to be taken literally, although I had no idea exactly what it was trying to tell me.

Nothing good, I was sure, even if I didn't think I needed to worry about receiving the unwelcome news that Max had offed himself overnight.

Thinking that a glass of water might help to rid myself of the dregs of the dream, I got out of bed and went down the hall to the bathroom. The house was too old to have an *en suite,* and the cost of knocking down walls and moving things around to create one would have been way too much for my renovation budget, most of which I'd blown on the ground-floor improvements.

Just as well. That walk down the hall helped to steady me a bit, as did the paper cup of cold water I poured for myself. I stared at my reflection in the mirror, ghostly and pale, since the only real illumination in the bathroom was a bit of moonlight slipping past the blinds.

Just what *had* the dream been trying to tell me? That there was going to be some sort of mishap on the set of *Perdition Row,* something involving a gun? Those horrible sorts of accidents did happen during filming every once in a while, although I knew massive precautions were taken on set to make sure everyone involved was as safe as possible.

I needed to warn Max. But how? It hadn't escaped my notice that he hadn't asked for my phone number when he came over on Saturday night, and so I sure hadn't been brave enough to ask for his.

Maybe he didn't ask because he didn't need to, I told myself, trying to be the voice of reason. *He could have gotten your number from his parents.*

True enough. Even so, that didn't help me much when it came to contacting him in case of an emergency.

Would Tina Sullivan give me her son's number? Her first impulse would probably be to give me his contact info without hesitation...unless Max had expressly forbidden it.

I wasn't sure I wanted to do that, though. If he really had told his mother not to give me his number, then I'd be putting her in an awkward position...to say the least...if I tried to get it from her.

All wasn't lost, though. I knew where he would be the next day. There was always the chance that the production's security guards wouldn't let me see him, but I'd have to take the risk. At the very least, I could ask them to pass along a note or something.

With the matter somewhat settled, I headed back to my bedroom and climbed under the covers once more. As I closed my eyes, I prayed I wouldn't dream.

Luckily, I didn't. Or, if more dreams floated up from my subconscious, I couldn't remember any of them, which was fine by me.

I had enough on my mind.

Just like the day before, I didn't sleep in very much, and so was ready to walk out the door by eight-thirty. Maybe that was too early, but I figured

I could always go and tidy up in the coffee shop for a bit until the crew started getting set up for that day's round of filming.

However, I discovered that Bridge Street was already blocked off by the time I got there at about a quarter to nine, and so I circled around the interdicted area and parked my Subaru in the space behind my building. Despite the early hour, there was a crowd of about a dozen people hanging out behind the barriers that had been set up to keep all onlookers safely away from the crew and the stars of the movie.

No sign of either Max or his director yet, though. That probably made some sense; there definitely wouldn't be any need for Max to be hanging around while they were still setting up the cameras and adjusting the lighting, although I would have thought Perry Lockhart would want to oversee the process. Maybe he left that sort of thing up to his director of photography. Not being an expert on movie set logistics, I couldn't say for sure.

But I did spot a big, burly guy wearing a black T-shirt with the word "security" printed on the back in large capital letters, just in case anyone couldn't figure out his job function merely by looking at him. I pulled in a breath of cool morning air, told myself I needed to do this no matter how self-conscious I felt, and walked up to the security guard.

"Hi," I said brightly as a frown settled on his thick brows. No doubt the scowl was his way of warning me off, but since I was here on a mission, I wouldn't let myself back down that easily. "I need to talk to Max Sullivan."

The security guard gave a brief, humorless laugh. "Yeah, you and the rest of them," he remarked with a dismissive glance toward the crowd of looky-loos.

Since I'd been expecting that sort of reply, I refused to let myself be deterred. "Just tell him it's Skye O'Malley. He knows me."

"Sure he does," the security guard scoffed.

"Look, just go tell him I need to see him," I said, hands now planted on my hips. "If he finds out I came by to see him and you sent me away, he's not going to be very happy."

For the first time, I thought I spied just the smallest hint of hesitation in the security guard's stance. He glanced away from me toward the place where Bridge Street curved around the plaza at the heart of town, and where several "Star Waggons" trailers had been set up. No doubt Max was in one of them, probably going over his lines or maybe just getting his makeup done.

After apparently doing some mental math and deciding it was probably better to ask, just in case Max and I were best buddies and not letting me in to see him could result in getting fired, the security guard unclipped the walkie-talkie from his belt and lifted it to his mouth. "Hey, Nat? I've got someone here who wants to talk to Mr. Sullivan. Says her name is Skye." A long pause, and then something that might have been grudging respect crossed the guy's heavy features. "Okay, he'll talk to you. One of the P.A.s will be over in a minute to take you to his trailer."

Thank God. It would have been nice if the security guard could have walked me over there instead of making me wait for a P.A., but I supposed the guy couldn't exactly leave his post, not when he had all those ravening hordes of Las Vegans to keep at bay...all ten or twelve of them.

A few minutes later, a short, thin woman around my own age of twenty-eight, with platinum-blonde hair cropped extra-close in a pixie cut, came over and eyed me briefly. She was very pretty, with a full mouth and dark eyes that gave the lie to her pale hair. "You're Skye?"

I nodded. "Yes, Max and I are old friends."

"So he said. Come on."

The woman hadn't bothered to introduce herself, but I wasn't about to stand on ceremony. No, I just followed her past a barricade and another security guard, this one even bigger and meaner-looking than the one who was babysitting the crowd on Bridge Street, and over to one of the Star

Waggons. She went up the steps, knocked on the door, and said, "Skye's here."

I didn't hear the response, but apparently Max had given the all-clear, because the P.A. said, "You can go on in. But don't take too long—we'll be shooting in fifteen minutes."

"No problem," I said. "I can make this quick."

She came back down the steps, and I ascended them, wondering if I should also knock. But no, she'd said I could go right in, so I just put my fingers on the handle and turned it before I stepped inside the trailer.

It seemed bigger on the inside than it had on the outside, with a lounge area directly where I'd entered, and then what appeared to be a makeup station with one of those fancy mirrors with lights all around it and a table cluttered with brushes and various pots of foundation and contour colors scattered across its surface. In front of the mirror was a director's chair, where Max was sitting. As soon as I began to move toward him, he got out of the chair and sent me a warm smile, although I thought I detected some confusion in his bright blue eyes.

"Skye," he said. "What's up? If you wanted a tour of the set, you could've just asked, you know."

Why did it not surprise me that he thought I was here for starstruck tourist reasons and nothing else?

If only it were that simple.

"I need to talk to you," I said, and something in the urgency of those words must have gotten through to him, because his smile faded.

"What's the matter?"

Now that we'd come to the moment, I wondered if I was even doing the right thing by coming here and trying to warn him. Not all of my dreams came true...especially the ones I wished for the most.

But enough of those oddly true dreams did become reality that I knew I couldn't ignore what I'd seen, or avoid passing on that information to Max. "I had a dream last night," I told him. "One of *those* dreams."

He didn't bother to ask what I meant by that. Max Sullivan might have been one of the least woo-woo people on the planet, but he knew about my dreams, knew how they turned out to be true at least seventy-five percent of the time. Those weren't the kind of odds most people would want to ignore.

"Let's sit down," he said, and gestured toward the lounge area near the door. "Do you want anything? Water? Coffee? It's not as good as your coffee, but—"

"Water is fine," I cut in. I'd already had a cup of French roast that morning, and besides, I was kind of a snob when it came to coffee. Most of the time, I wouldn't drink anything I hadn't made.

One corner of his mouth quirked a bit, as if he knew exactly why I'd refused anything caffeinated. Instead, he went to a small fridge tucked into a corner of the trailer and pulled out two bottles of Perrier. "I hope fizzy is okay," he said as he handed me one.

"It's fine," I assured him.

Still smiling a little, he took a seat on the sectional, and so I went ahead and sat down a few feet away. This close, I could see the makeup he wore in preparation for that day's filming, not heavy or anything, but enough to smooth everything out and make sure he wouldn't be shiny on camera.

"So," he said, after unscrewing the cap of his Perrier and taking a swig, "what was this dream you had?"

I didn't know whether the Perrier would lend me courage, but I figured it couldn't hurt. After swallowing some of the carbonated water, I said, "Well, at first, it didn't seem that strange. The two of us were sitting on the porch swing and talking. But then...."

"Then?" he prompted.

Looking at him now, I realized he was wearing the same getup he'd had on in my dream—a band-collared linen shirt, heavy linen pants with suspenders...a belt at his waist from which dangled a holster.

In that holster was a revolver.

I swallowed. I couldn't see all of the gun, of course, but that pearl handle looked familiar, as did the gleam of nickel along its surface.

"What's wrong?" Max asked. His gaze seemed to follow where I was staring, and a friendly grin crinkled the skin around his bright blue eyes. "The gun? Don't worry—it's just a prop."

A prop? For a second or two, I floundered, wondering if I'd been mistaken about the whole thing. Surely a prop gun couldn't be an issue, could it?

Somehow, I managed to find my voice. "I saw it in my dream."

The smile abruptly disappeared. "This gun? This same gun?"

"I think so."

He unsnapped the holster and pulled out the revolver. Yes, that was definitely the same weapon I'd seen in my dream, right down to the gorgeously intricate engraving along the barrel. It was hard to believe it wasn't real. "You're sure?"

I nodded. "Yes, I'm sure. I saw you pick it up and, well...point it at yourself."

Those words got me a couple of severely lifted eyebrows. "I *shot* myself?"

"I think so," I said, then quickly amended, "That is, I woke up right then, so I don't know for sure what happened next. But it was disturbing, to say the least. And right before you pointed the gun at your head, you'd been talking about how you didn't like working with guns, how there was always the potential for something to go wrong. That's why I needed to come down here and talk to you, make sure everything was okay."

In silence, he returned the prop gun to its holster and secured it. "Everything's fine," he said, his tone supremely confident, even though what I'd just told him should have shaken him a bit. Then again, he was an actor; maybe he had been knocked a little off balance by my story but wasn't about to show it. "Actually, we aren't even doing any live shooting today. The real gun—the one they copied to make this prop version—is safely locked up off set."

"But you will be doing live shooting at some point, right?" I persisted, knowing I probably sounded a little too desperate.

"Next week," Max said. "Out on location, nowhere close to downtown. It'll be completely safe—you know I know how to handle a gun. And even if I didn't," he went on, not giving me a chance to respond, "we've got a bunch of experts on set to make sure everything goes exactly right. There's no chance in hell there could be some kind of accidental shooting, or whatever it was that your dream was trying to warn you about."

Well, at least he hadn't said I was crazy for

coming to him with this talk of dreams. In the past, he'd had every reason to believe me, since he'd seen the evidence of those dreams' accuracy for himself. After being away for so many years, though, he might have decided it was all a lot of hooey, an attention-getting device dreamed up by the awkward girl next door.

That didn't seem to be the case, though, and I knew I should be grateful he seemed to be taking me seriously.

"It might not have such a literal interpretation," I said. "Sometimes it takes a while for a dream's meaning to percolate through. I guess I just wanted to make sure you're being careful."

The smile was back, this time accompanied by what Max probably had intended as a reassuring pat on my arm. Now, though, even that brief, friendly contact was enough to send a little shiver through me. Was this the first time we'd ever touched, other than when we'd roughhoused as little kids?

I thought so. I had to believe I would have remembered if there had been a similar moment sometime before this one.

"I'm always careful," he replied. "Come on—all these action movies, and I've never even broken a bone. It's all good."

Oh, how I wished I could believe him. Not that he wasn't careful, since his history of escaping all those wild and woolly shoot-'em-up movies with nothing more than a few scrapes and bruises to show for his trouble was pretty well documented, but I didn't know whether things were actually "all good."

If they were, I wouldn't have had that dream.

"I know," I said, and then stopped, because a knock came at the door, and the P.A.'s platinum-blonde head popped inside the trailer.

"Five minutes, Max," she told him in warning tones as she compressed her perfectly lacquered mouth, and then disappeared again.

Looking resigned, he said, "We should probably wrap this up—"

"It's fine," I broke in. The last thing I wanted was to make him late. "I just thought I should let you know what I saw."

"And I appreciate it."

He was smiling, once again looking as though he didn't have a care in the world. If the details of my dream had troubled him at all, you wouldn't know it to look at him.

I told him goodbye, then let myself out. As I was descending the steps from the trailer, the door to the Star Waggon across the street opened, and Lauralee Peters came out, flaxen hair styled into perfect 1930s finger waves, a silky bias-cut dress showing off every inch of her slender, sylph-like figure.

No comparisons, no comparisons, went furiously through my brain, even though I couldn't quite prevent myself from looking down at my jeans and black T-shirt, my black sandals.

Well, at least my toes were done.

I didn't go home right away, though. After popping in to the coffee shop's storeroom to make sure Tilly had adequate food and water—she'd eaten a lot of the stuff I'd put out earlier, so it was good that I'd checked—I went back out to Bridge Street to join the group of onlookers, figuring it couldn't hurt to watch some of the filming. Yes, Max had said they wouldn't be doing any live firing today...which made sense, since I doubted the looky-loos would have been allowed anywhere close if the actors and crew were working with live ammunition...but it just seemed smart to get the lay of the land.

If nothing else, it would be interesting to see how he and Perry Lockhart interacted.

Not very well, as it turned out. True, I'd gotten the impression that Perry didn't get along with basically anyone, but still, you had to be a special species of jerk to irritate Max, whose cheerful disposition required a lot of stirring up before you started to see any cracks in his sunny façade. Today, though, it seemed he couldn't do anything right, as Perry kept calling, "Cut!" before Max was even able to get up a head of steam.

After about fifteen minutes of this, I decided I'd had enough and headed home. The last thing I wanted was to watch my old friend get humiliated, especially since it appeared to me Perry was going out of his way to deride pretty much everything Max did. It also didn't help that he was much kinder to Lauralee Peters, and didn't even call her out the one time she obviously flubbed her lines.

Playing favorites?

It sure seemed that way. Maybe Perry hadn't wanted to work with Max at all, had wanted more of an actor's actor for the role, rather than someone who'd made a name in big action movies and fluffy rom-coms. Since I knew very little about studio politics, I really couldn't guess at the reason behind the director's noticeably foul attitude.

Whatever was going on, it sure looked to me like my friend was going to earn every cent of the fifteen million or so he was getting paid for the role.

The whole experience had left a bad taste in my mouth, so after I got home, I made up a batch of strawberry lemonade and had a glass while sitting at the kitchen table and watching the day's fresh breeze play with the flowers in the yard. Once I was done with my lemonade, I decided to head over to the community garden down the block and pull up some weeds. If nothing else, the activity might help me to work out some of my animosity toward Perry Lockhart, a man who clearly had no problem running over people's psyches and then backing up and running over them again just to make sure he hadn't missed anything.

My grandmother had been the motivating force behind the community garden—a home had once stood on the half-acre plot of land, but it had been abandoned and turned into quite the eyesore. She'd gotten together with the neighbors, and everyone had pooled their resources to buy the property so it could become a communal place where each person who had a stake could cultivate their own little corner and grow whatever they liked. That was why our backyard had always been a riot of flowers and very little that was culinary, since we mainly planted our veggies and herbs in the community space, a tradition I kept up even after she'd passed.

Luckily, the weather had cooled a bit, and so the day was pleasantly warm rather than fiercely hot. I pulled weeds and gathered herbs, and eyeballed the tomatoes, guessing some of them were definitely ready to go home with me. I picked the most likely tomatoes and put them in the basket I'd brought along, allowing myself a momentary fantasy of Max actually following up on his comment about inviting me to the ranch, and how I'd bring the tomatoes over and whip up a batch of marinara right there on the spot.

Well, they did say the way to a man's heart was through his stomach.

By the time I was done, my ire toward Perry Lockhart had cooled a bit. Not all the way, because no amount of sunshine and fresh air would change my opinion that the guy was an irredeemable jerk, but at least I'd worked off most of my desire to march over and give him a good smack upside the head. Anyway, Max was a big boy and definitely didn't need me defending him.

No phone call from him that evening, though, which made me less than happy. However, I reminded myself that he'd had a rough day and was probably too tired to be making any social overtures. And although he hadn't asked, I was pretty sure he'd gotten a full update from his mother about me, and so he must know I wasn't seeing anyone at the moment. My current single state had probably made him think it was just fine to wait until Saturday to get in touch, since my social calendar wasn't exactly what you could call full.

On Saturday morning, I did my usual puttering about, although there wasn't quite as much to putter with, considering I'd had the two preceding days as well to do any necessary odds and ends around the house. When the phone rang a little after ten-thirty, I couldn't quite hold back a shiver of anticipation. Maybe Max had decided he really should reach out if he wanted to see me that night.

I didn't recognize the phone number when I looked down at my cell phone's screen, but the number displayed there had a 310 area code, which I vaguely recalled was somewhere in California.

It just had to be him.

"Skye?"

Yes, that was definitely Max's voice, although he sounded tired and strained, and not at all like himself.

"Hi, Max," I said. "What's up?"

A long pause. "Someone shot Perry Lockhart last night."

Cold washed through me...even as I had a flash of Max holding the gun to his head in that awful dream of mine...but I managed to say in what I thought were reasonably calm tones, "That's terrible."

I couldn't see Max's face, of course, but I got the feeling he smiled grimly. "It gets better," he responded. "Chief DeVargas thinks I did it."

CHAPTER 6

Cloud of Suspicion

Well, I'd made it over to Sunset Ridge, the ranch Max was renting, but I definitely could never have imagined it would be under these circumstances. We sat out on the patio, a huge expanse of flagstone pavers with views that went on forever, while a soft breeze faintly scented with dry grass ruffled our hair.

However, I couldn't quite allow myself to enjoy my surroundings, not after receiving such horrible news.

"Did you have to post bail?" I asked.

"I haven't been formally charged yet," Max replied as he nursed a Dos Equis. And okay, some might have said that ten forty-five in the morning was a little early for day drinking, but I thought he could be excused, considering the circumstances.

"But Chief DeVargas made it sound as though it was only a matter of time."

That comment made me want to shake my head, but I refrained. Marie DeVargas had been the chief of police in Las Vegas for the past five years, and although I'd never had to deal with her directly, everything I'd heard from Kyle Isaacs and other people in the community made it sound as though she was tough but fair, the kind of person who wasn't likely to jump to conclusions.

No, she would need proof...strong proof... before she ever considered recommending that someone should be charged with murder.

"Why is she focused on you?" I asked next. Unlike Max, I was drinking plain old water. Or not so plain—he'd poured me a glass of Evian from a big bottle he had in the fridge, and added a lemon slice. Even under extreme duress, he knew how to be a gracious host. But I supposed that was one of the things I loved about him, that he was able to roll with whatever life might throw his way.

He set down his bottle of beer and ran a hand through his hair, gaze fixed toward the west, where our hometown lay—and where the police station was located, although of course you couldn't see it from our current spot. "Because mine were the only fingerprints on the gun."

Even though the air was already warm,

signaling another hot day on the way, a little shiver of cold moved down my spine. In my mind's eye, I saw the gun from my dream, the one whose prop version Max had been wearing as part of his costume the day before, and I just *knew*.

Still, I thought I'd better ask.

"Your gun?" I said. "The one from my dream?"

He nodded and retrieved his bottle of beer, took another swallow. "Yeah, that one." His expression turned uncharacteristically bitter as he added, "I guess I should've listened to you."

What was I supposed to say to that remark? I'd done my best to warn him, but my dream hadn't shown me anything about Perry getting shot, or that Max might be accused of his murder. No, it had only provided vague warnings about a gun being dangerous, which was pretty basic information when you got right down to it.

"I still think it sounds like some flimsy evidence," I told him. "Of course your fingerprints would be on the gun—it's a prop you would use all the time while filming." I paused there. "I mean, you have picked it up, right? You've used it?"

A brief nod. "Yes, I did some practice shooting with it last week. I needed to make sure I could handle it properly for the scenes where we'd be live firing."

So much for my hope that he might not have

touched the real gun at all, had only handled the prop version. All the same....

"It still doesn't mean much that yours are the only prints on the gun," I told him. "I mean, all someone would have to do is wear gloves when they handled it to avoid messing with the evidence."

"Yeah, I know," Max said. There was the slightest edge to his voice, although I could tell he was doing his best to keep it together. "And I tried to tell Chief DeVargas that. But all she said was that they were investigating and that I needed to be available for further questioning." He stopped there and fixed me with a direct look, his blue gaze now almost pleading. "Skye, I didn't do it, but I don't know how to prove that. It sounds like Perry was shot at his vacation rental sometime in the middle of the night, and I was alone here, asleep. Pretty crappy alibi, huh?"

Unfortunately, it was. At the same time, I couldn't quite hold back a small inner sense of relief. If Max had been here by himself, then he clearly wasn't spending time with his costar. To be fair, the two of them had both vehemently denied the rumors of an affair, but still, getting confirmation that he'd spent the night alone was at least a further corroboration that absolutely nothing was going on between them.

But if he'd been with Lauralee Peters all night, at least she would have been able to verify his whereabouts, could have told Chief DeVargas there was no way he could be Perry Lockhart's murderer.

I held back a sigh of my own. This was all absolutely crazy.

"Why would the chief even think you had a motive?" I asked, knowing I needed to stay on track. "I thought you were super-excited to be working with Perry. None of this makes any sense."

"I know, right?" Max returned, the quasi-rhetorical question accompanied by another swallow of beer. "Problem is, we didn't have the best working relationship."

"Well, true," I said, recalling with painful clarity the way the director had berated my friend during yesterday morning's shoot.

Max shot me a quizzical glance. "How would you know anything about that?"

A guilty flush crept up my cheeks despite my best efforts to hold it back. "Um...I might have hung around a while after we talked yesterday. I thought it would be interesting to watch the filming for a little while."

Max's expression went curiously blank, as though he wanted to make sure he didn't let slip any betraying tells. "So...you saw that."

"Some of it," I replied. "Honestly, I got

disgusted pretty quick and left. I don't know how you can put up with that crap on a daily basis."

"Neither does Chief DeVargas," Max said, now sounding almost resigned. "Which is why she thinks I killed Perry. She thinks I couldn't take it anymore, lost my temper, and shot him."

On the surface, that theory sounded barely plausible...if you didn't know Max. I could see him getting fed up enough that he might quit, walking away from any award opportunities and possibly inviting a lawsuit...depending on his contract...but to shoot someone in cold blood?

It was ridiculous.

"Well, then, she doesn't know you very well," I said, and he almost smiled.

"No, she doesn't. Actually, she doesn't have any reason to know me at all—I think this is the first time I've ever even met her."

Which made sense. Marie DeVargas was a local, the same as Max and me, but she was in her late forties, definitely not someone we would have gone to school with or interacted with at all. She came into the coffee shop on rare occasions, and so she and I had exchanged a few pleasantries about the weather or whatever. Max, on the other hand, wasn't the kind of guy who'd gotten in trouble during high school, and so he wouldn't have run afoul of her when she was just a deputy and starting out with the Las Vegas P.D.

He paused and drank some beer, a much more modest swallow than the previous ones, as though his nerves were starting to steady down now that we'd been talking a bit. "To be fair, Chief DeVargas was almost apologetic. Said she'd seen all my movies and was a fan, but it didn't change the fact that I was currently the only person of interest in the case."

How polite of her. I reached for my glass of lemon water and took a sip, then sat there for a moment, pondering. A sudden thought struck me, and I asked, "How do they even know it's murder? Maybe Perry shot himself."

Max's eyebrows lifted. "If you'd met Perry Lockhart, you'd know he was the last person in the world to commit suicide."

"I *did* meet him," I said, and Max shot me a startled look. "I mean, he came into the shop to get a double espresso and acted like a complete tool."

Now appearing almost resigned, he said, "Par for the course. Sorry about that."

I shrugged. "No need for you to apologize for your director's behavior. Anyway, I could tell he was a self-important jerk, so yeah, he didn't strike me as the sort of person who would decide to take his own life. Then again, you never know what's going on in people's heads."

For a second or two, Max was quiet, apparently thinking over my words. Then his brows drew together, and he said, "While it's a convenient theory, I doubt it's going to pan out. Chief DeVargas didn't go into the gory details or anything, but she did say Perry had been shot in the chest when he was found in the middle of the living room at his Airbnb. If someone's trying to kill themselves, they generally don't put a bullet through their heart."

Oh. I didn't pretend to be an expert on the subject, but it did seem pretty clear this wasn't a case of suicide. And while I appreciated Max calling me and asking for my input—probably because he was more rattled by my semi-prophetic dream than he wanted to admit—I also thought we should probably address the elephant in the room.

"Um...Max, shouldn't you be talking to a lawyer about all this?"

To my surprise, he grinned then, looking much more like his usual insouciant self. "Oh, I did," he said. "That is, I called my personal lawyer, and he's reaching out to a criminal defense attorney, since his specialty is entertainment law. Right now, I'm waiting to hear who he's found. I just figured that in the meantime, I might as well get some input from the woman whose dream told her something bad was going to happen with that damn gun."

His reply settled my unease a bit. It was quite possible that his lawyer would read him the riot act for discussing all this stuff with someone who wasn't directly involved in the case, but I didn't see the harm in being Max's sounding board. If his lawyer—whoever that turned out to be—ended up telling him he needed to stay quiet and let the experts handle this, then I'd butt out.

In the meantime, though, I had to admit being more cheered than I probably should be at the prospect of being his confidante.

A swallow of lemon water to fortify myself, and then I said, "Okay, let's look at this logically. Who else had access to the gun?"

"Jon Hansford—he's the armorer," Max replied at once. "And Letty Mendoza...she's the prop master. No one else, though. On a day when we would be live firing, Jon would lock up the gun afterward in a portable safe and hand it over to Letty."

At least it sounded as though they were being responsible with the firearm. "No one else?"

Max drummed his fingers against one knee, then shook his head. "Not that I'm aware of. Letty kept the safe in a locked storage unit the production's renting here in town. That's where it was on Friday, since I was using the prop version for the scenes we were shooting here downtown."

A storage unit wasn't exactly Fort Knox, but it still wasn't anything that would be terribly easy to access, either. I found myself frowning as I said,

"Do you know who else might have keys to that storage unit?"

"Perry probably did," Max replied. "Or maybe one of the producers. I really don't know all the logistics that went on behind the scenes. I just remember Letty and Jon taking care of securing all the firearms we were using during the shoot."

Not for the first time, I reflected that was an unfortunate word to describe the process of filming a movie, especially considering how Perry Lockhart had died.

Brushing the thought aside, I said, "Do you know whether Letty or Jon would have any kind of a grudge against Perry?"

Max's response was immediate. "I doubt it. I mean, I know Jon's worked with him on a bunch of different films. And Letty—she's local. I think the producers hired her because they were trying to show they'd made an effort at diversity when it came to staffing the crew."

"Local, local?" I asked, even as I wracked my brains, trying to remember if I'd ever met anyone named Letty. The name didn't ring a bell.

"Not from Las Vegas," Max replied, now looking almost amused. "I think I heard she's from Albuquerque, or maybe someplace south of there. Belen?" Before I could say anything, his shoulders lifted and he continued. "I just meant she wasn't from L.A. like a lot of the crew. But since she was recently hired and doesn't seem to have any kind of a history with Perry, I find it hard to believe she'd have any reason to shoot him."

Great. Here I'd been hoping this would turn out to be an open-and-shut case, but it didn't seem we were going to be that lucky.

"Well, someone obviously got that gun out of the safe," I said, and Max's mouth tightened.

"I know. But there could be something else going on here, something I just can't think of at the moment. Maybe some of the producers had access to the safe as well. Considering what a pain in the ass Perry was to work with, I don't think it's impossible that one of them might have decided they were done dealing with his crap."

That would be a handy solution to the problem, for it to be revealed that Perry's death was the result of some particularly nasty entertainment industry infighting and Max had absolutely nothing to do with it.

However, if that turned out to be the case, I didn't see how I would ever be able to prove it. I wasn't a member of the Las Vegas police department, or even a private detective or a lawyer, someone who might be able to get access to the sorts of high-powered people I imagined Hollywood producers must be.

No, I was just a woman who owned a coffee shop in a small town most people had never heard of, someone who sometimes had weirdly prophetic dreams or saw significant patterns in tea leaves. While those odd qualities had helped me out a time or two in the past, I didn't see how they would be of much assistance right now.

Max must have noted some darkening of my expression, because he said, "I'm not expecting you to go grill the producers about their relationship with Perry or anything like that."

"You're not?" I asked, trying not to sound too relieved.

"Of course not. I wanted to talk to you because you're someone I can trust."

"I am?" I responded.

A look of surprise flitted across his face, as if he was startled I would even ask such a question.

"Sure you are," he said, voice as confident as one of the heroes he portrayed, like he'd just delivered a line about how he was sure he'd be able to defuse that bomb. "You've always been someone I could talk to. You were never like some of those girls in high school, gossiping and plotting and doing whatever they could to make sure their clique stayed on top."

Now it was my turn to look surprised. Oh, there had definitely been girls like that at our high school—among them, his ex-girlfriend Raylene— but I suppose I'd never thought he'd been paying any particular attention to all the petty power plays the girls at our school had indulged in. Max had always seemed like someone who sailed above all that stuff, liked by everyone, star of the football team and the debate team, the guy who always got the lead in the school plays. That he would have even noticed how some of the girls who ran in his crowd weren't exactly the nicest people in the world came as something of a shock.

"Um...thanks," I replied, since I really didn't know what else to say.

He smiled then, and picked up his bottle of beer. "I know you won't tell anyone what we've said here. And I suppose I was also hoping maybe you could do a little tea leaf reading or whatever, maybe dig up some stuff that's not exactly visible to the naked eye, if you know what I mean."

There it was. I knew I was probably being naïve to think he wouldn't ask me to do a reading on the subject, since I wasn't exactly the kind of psychic... if you could even call me a psychic at all...who read palms or Tarot cards, or who looked into a crystal ball or channeled the spirits of her ancestors for enlightenment. No, for whatever reason, those little bits and pieces of leaf stuck to the side or bottom of a cup were what had decided to reveal the universe to me, and even then, their signals could be just a little bit murky.

"It's not what you can exactly call foolproof—" I began.

"I'm not asking for foolproof," Max cut in, although once again, he was smiling a little, his manner as relaxed and easy as though he was simply asking me for a custom brew back at my coffee shop. Then he sent me a considering look. "How accurate are your readings these days, anyway?"

A helpless little shrug lifted my shoulders. "I don't know...maybe seventy-five, eighty percent."

His smile broadened. "I'd call those good odds. Better than what my investment advisers can do." He leaned forward, elbows resting on his thighs, expression earnest. "I'm just asking you to give it a try. What could it hurt?"

Good question. Most of the time when people asked me to read the leaves for them, it was for relationship advice, or maybe requesting clarification on a particular decision they needed to make. I was always very clear that the tea leaves only offered suggestions, not concrete medical or financial guidance, and most people were fine with that.

But I'd never used the leaves to help me find a murderer, and I honestly didn't know whether they'd be up to the task. This was a whole heck of a lot more complicated than trying to decide whether to remodel your house or just list the place and move on to a new home.

"This is your life we're talking about, Max," I said. "The last thing I want is to tell you something that turns out to be dead wrong, or gets you in even more trouble."

"You wouldn't do that," he said with a smile.

I wondered what it was like to be so confident, so sure that every step you took was the right one. Lord knows I'd been second-guessing myself pretty much my entire life, always wondering maybe if I'd been smarter or prettier or more talented, my father might have thought I was enough and wouldn't have spent all those years after my mother left us slowly drinking himself into an early grave, as though he believed that with her gone, there just wasn't much left to keep him around.

Including his daughter.

"Not on purpose," I said quietly, hoping the intensity of my tone might get through to Max even though my words didn't seem to be doing too good a job of penetrating his vision of me as some kind of all-seeing eye. "But these sorts of things are always open to interpretation, and if they're interpreted wrong...." I let the words trail off and made myself look directly into his clear blue eyes, an almost perfect echo of the sunny skies above us. "I just don't want you to follow my advice and end up in even worse trouble."

Now he leaned back against the padded cushion of the love seat where he'd been sitting, his expression far less troubled than I would have liked.

"It's kind of hard to think of something worse than being accused of first-degree murder."

Well, he had a point there. All the same, I clearly needed to be the voice of caution in this situation, because otherwise, he seemed ready to grasp at anything that might give him the answers he wanted to hear.

"True," I allowed. "And I'm not saying I won't do it. I'm just saying you need to look before you leap."

Something he'd never been very good at. Max Sullivan was the kind of guy who always strode blithely into the unknown, certain there would always be a net to catch him the second he slid off the tightrope. I'd always admired...and maybe envied...that quality about him, especially since I often felt like his polar opposite, someone who was never quite sure of herself.

"I will," he said earnestly. "And I'm not saying I'm not going to take the advice of the lawyer Philip finds for me, whoever he or she turns out to be. But I figured it couldn't hurt to have a little supernatural help on my side, especially since you're the one who first got the idea that something bad was about to go down on the *Perdition Row* shoot."

Those words made me feel a little better about the situation. Maybe Max had acquired some wisdom along the way, had realized that going in with guns blazing—pardon the expression—wasn't always the best course of action.

My silence didn't seem to bother him much, because his eyes lit up with amusement when he spoke again.

"Help me, Skye O'Malley—you're my only hope."

CHAPTER 7

Getting Gritty

Deanne appeared on my doorstep a few hours after I came home from Max's rented ranch. Although I'd assured him that I'd brew some tea when I got home and see what I could find, I hadn't quite steeled myself yet to do the deed.

What if the tea leaves were all too clear, and told me he really *had* killed Perry Lockhart?

I told myself that was impossible, that Max Sullivan was no more a murderer than I was. The past ten years—and his enormous success—didn't seem to have changed him all that much, and so I couldn't even use the excuse that he was a different man from the boy he used to be, and so my current estimation of his character might not be terribly accurate.

Anyway, I messed around for a while in the

backyard, pulling weeds, doing my weekly whack at the carpet of morning glories that covered the back fence so they wouldn't encroach into the neighbor's yard, and then headed inside to put in a load of laundry. Anything to avoid brewing a batch of tea to see what it would reveal. I knew Max was waiting to hear from me, but I hadn't given him an exact time, had only said I'd sit down and read the leaves when the time felt right. Luckily, he hadn't questioned that admittedly woo-woo statement, but had only said that was fine, he wasn't going anywhere.

That was for sure. Chief DeVargas had apparently told him not to leave town. But since she'd also issued the same order to the rest of the *Perdition Row* cast and crew, I harbored the faint hope that the police chief hadn't yet decided Max was the only possible suspect. The situation might change as soon as she talked to the D.A. on Monday morning, but in the meantime, it seemed everyone was in sort of a holding pattern.

And it also meant that everyone would be sticking around in the interim. Max hadn't said anything about what was going on with the rest of the crew, or his fellow cast members, but I had to believe everyone must be in an uproar. What would happen next, I had no idea. Would the producers bring in another director to pick up where Perry had left off? That seemed like the most reasonable thing to do, but maybe their funding was contingent on having Perry Lockhart at the helm.

So many questions...so few answers.

Anyway, because I was standing in the living room and watering the plants there, I didn't have any way of pretending I wasn't home. No doubt Deanne had driven over and then knocked on the front door because she'd guessed I was purposely avoiding my phone.

"So, when *exactly* were you going to tell me?" she demanded as she marched inside.

Wearily, I closed the door and turned back to face my friend. She had her hands on her hips and an expression of something close to outrage on her pixie-like features.

"It sounds as though you've already heard about the whole mess through the grapevine," I said as I set my watering can down on the living room rug.

Deanne didn't seem terribly convinced by that argument, since her eyes narrowed slightly. "Well, true, but still!"

"I guess I'm still just trying to process everything," I said. "But let's go in the kitchen. I could use a glass of iced tea. How about you?"

For a moment, I wondered whether she was going to call out my invitation as the obvious stalling tactic it was, but then she seemed to relent, saying, "Sure, sounds good."

I retrieved the watering can and headed back to the kitchen, then set it down on the counter and proceeded to get out a couple of glasses and the pitcher of sun tea I kept in the fridge. The kitchen was a big, homey one with a table and chairs set near one of the windows so you could sit there and look out into the backyard as you had your morning coffee or ate breakfast or whatever. I led Deanne over to the table, then handed her one of the glasses I was holding.

"He didn't do it," I said as we both sat down.

"Well, of *course* he didn't," she responded, as if that should have been patently obvious. "Does he have any idea who might have done it?"

"No," I said, and her face fell. "And now Max seems to think I can find out who actually did kill Perry Lockhart just by reading some tea leaves or something."

This comment didn't seem to faze my friend, because she said, "Well, can't you?"

I couldn't quite prevent myself from rolling my eyes. "It doesn't work like that, Deanne."

She lifted her glass of sun tea and took a sip before saying, "Then, how does it work?"

"By giving me hints, small things to think about. It's not like the tea leaves are going to spell out the name of the killer or something."

Judging by the way her head tilted as she considered my reply, she didn't appear terribly put off by my underwhelming response. "Well, a hint is better than nothing, isn't it?"

"I suppose so," I allowed, although I wasn't going to give her much more affirmation than that.

For a few seconds, she didn't say anything, only sipped some more tea. Then her eyes lit up, and she said, "But he called you, didn't he? I mean, of all the people in town he could have reached out to, he wanted to talk to you. That's got to mean something."

"It means Max knows I'm the only person in Las Vegas who reads tea leaves," I said. Maybe a similar thought had crossed my mind, but I knew better than to get my hopes up and believe we might have a life together that included something a little more than the relationship we now had. Clearly, he looked on me as a trusted friend...and yet I also knew he didn't see me as anything other than that.

Whether he'd change his mind at a later date remained to be seen.

"The only person he trusts who also reads tea leaves," she corrected me, just a smidge too much triumph in her tone. I had to say this for my friend —she was eternally hopeful, even when the situation didn't appear to merit too much hope. And she'd always believed that one day Max would figure out what he was missing by not being with me, even though our prospects for a shared future had seemed pretty remote after he relocated to Los Angeles.

"Well, I think we should probably put that aside for now," I said. "Whatever Max Sullivan does or doesn't think of me, the most important thing is to figure out who actually killed Perry Lockhart. Otherwise, Max could be in real trouble."

Deanne's expression was dubious. "Are you really sure about that, though? I mean, I have to believe he can afford an army of lawyers."

"He can," I allowed. "But all the lawyers in the world won't do any good if the only piece of real physical evidence points to him being the one person with motive and whose fingerprints were found on the murder weapon."

Because my best friend didn't flinch or act at all surprised by that comment, I had to believe she'd also heard about that part of the story. News sure traveled fast around here. It was hard to say who'd spilled the beans, but I had my suspicions.

"Well," she said, "it shouldn't be too hard to figure out who else had a motive. From what I've heard, that Perry guy sounded like a real jerk." A flicker of remorse moved across her features, and she quickly added, "Not to speak ill of the dead or anything."

"It's okay," I replied, since I'd thought the same thing multiple times. "He *was* a jerk. But lots of people go on being jerks every single day without getting shot over it, so I have to believe there must be some other reason." I paused there, then said, "The hard part is going to be figuring out what that is."

Deanne hung out at the house for another half-hour or so, then excused herself, saying she needed to run by the store on her way home so she could pick up a few odds and ends for dinner. Under normal circumstances, she might have invited me over, but I think she picked up on my vibe that I wanted to be alone that evening.

Well, what I really wanted was for Max to invite me back over to the ranch so we could discuss his predicament some more. However, since he hadn't called, I had to believe he was feeling the same need to be on his own that I was.

Or maybe he just didn't want to bug me or do anything that would keep me from reading the leaves and getting some kind of much-needed clue.

Now that I was by myself again, I really didn't have any more excuse not to at least attempt a reading. Dutifully, I filled the teapot with filtered water from the Brita pitcher I always kept in a sheltered spot on the counter and turned up the gas on the stove, then headed into the pantry to peruse the containers of tea I kept there, wondering which one to use for this all-important bit of divination. Most of the time, I either used oolong or one of my own proprietary herbal blends, but considering the nature of this particular request, I thought some gunpowder green tea might work best.

I brought the container over to the counter and then got down the cup and saucer I always used for my divinations. You could buy special tasseography cups with arcane symbols painted on the interior and saucer, but I didn't bother with anything like that. No, I used one of my grandmother's old cups, a pretty piece of porcelain with cheerful yellow and pink and blue flowers painted on the exterior, and the sort of nice, flared shape that worked best for tea leaf readings.

A half teaspoon of some gunpowder tea in the cup, and then I brought in one of the vanilla-scented candles that usually sat on the sideboard in the dining room and set it down on the kitchen table. I lit the candle and let the soft, sweet aroma begin to fill the room. At the same time, I did my best to breathe in deeply and allow myself to relax. Being stressed out and jangly was pretty much a guarantee I wouldn't get any kind of an accurate reading.

The water in the kettle began to boil, and I quickly shut off the gas and waited a moment for it to settle down a bit. Once I judged it was hot but not actively bubbling, I poured the heated water over the leaves, then took the cup and saucer over to the kitchen table where the vanilla candle was already placidly burning, the sweet scent helping to calm my nerves a bit. The table had always been my favorite location to perform this ritual, a tranquil spot where I could look down at the backyard and all the cheerful flowers there, where I could let the shimmering movements of the oaks and cottonwoods along the edge of the garden work their own kind of magic in my soul.

Another few minutes to let the tea steep—this definitely wasn't a ritual for the hasty—and then I lifted the cup and allowed myself one very small sip to test the temperature. It was hot, but not so extreme I had to worry about burning my tongue, and so I swallowed a little more, gradually working my way through the cup as I watched the wind play with the leaves on the trees and the carefully tended roses and dahlias and hollyhocks. I knew I needed to allow myself this space to let my mind open to the strange gift I'd supposedly inherited from my great-grandmother, or this would all be in vain.

When there was only a teaspoon or so of liquid left in the cup, I held it in front of me and swirled the remaining tea three times, again doing my best to focus on the question I needed to have answered.

Who really killed Perry Lockhart?

That part of the ritual satisfied, I placed the

saucer over the cup and then turned the cup upside down, letting the remaining tea dribble onto the saucer. With the handle facing toward me, I turned the teacup right side up and gazed down into it, briefly noting that none of the leaves had been left on the saucer.

Well, that simplified things a bit.

However, it was definitely crowded inside that cup. I stared down into it for a moment, still concentrating on my question. To my dismay, the leaves were mostly a jumbled mess, doing their best to hide the answer I was seeking.

There, though...almost directly opposite me, and standing off on its own from the rest of the sodden leaves, was a little blob shaped like a heart.

A heart?

In tea-leaf reading, a heart often meant exactly what you'd think it would—love, a lover coming into your life, whatever. If it had an arrow pointing through it, the symbol could be negative, depending on which way it was pointing, but there was no arrow here. Just a perfectly formed little heart stuck to the porcelain.

Okay, then. I sat back in my chair and continued to stare into the cup, doing my best not to be flummoxed. The appearance of a heart could signal Perry's death had been the result of some sort of lover's quarrel, although that quarrel must have been with someone other than Max. I might not have been in his life these past ten years, but I knew he hadn't changed *that* much.

Then again, Max had told me that Perry had been shot through the heart. Maybe the tea leaves were being extra-literal today and were simply pointing out an obvious fact of the case.

The more I thought about it, though, the more that particular theory didn't make much sense. I'd asked about who had killed Perry, not how he had died. There was clearly something else going on here.

All right...maybe Perry had been involved with someone in the cast or crew, and they'd shot him when he dumped them, or treated them cruelly in some other way. While this scenario seemed plausible enough—I kind of doubted Perry Lockhart was the sort of person to worry about the tender feelings of his romantic partners—it still left me with the problem of who exactly would have even had access to that locked-up gun to carry out their revenge.

Had Perry been sleeping with Letty, the prop master? That theory seemed kind of far-fetched, but at the moment, it made more sense than anything else, just because she was one of the few people on the crew who could easily get her hands on the film's weaponry, and getting burned by her director and lover would have definitely provided the necessary motive.

Or maybe Perry Lockhart had been having an affair with Jon, the armorer. Max had told me the two of them had worked on a lot of films together, so maybe it was a long-term kind of thing, the sort of liaison that could turn pretty toxic if one of the parties involved decided to end things. True, Perry had struck me as pretty hetero, but I'd be the first person to admit my gaydar wasn't exactly what you could call well-developed.

Either way, it seemed as though a lot more intelligence-gathering would be needed to illuminate the tea leaves' muddy clues. How exactly I was supposed to manage that, though, I didn't have the foggiest idea. It wasn't as though I had access to the cast and crew, and if I showed up at the Plaza Hotel and started asking pointed questions, I'd be sure to raise people's suspicions almost immediately.

Then again....

Okay, raiding the Plaza wasn't in the cards. On the other hand, I owned a business only a block away, the sort of place where people would drop in to get some coffee or a snack, if for no other reason than they desperately wanted a change of scenery.

And yes, Levitation Latte wasn't open on Sundays, but I doubted the *Perdition Row* cast and crew knew that. Even if they noted the discrepancy between the hours posted on the coffee shop window and the obvious fact of the place being open when it shouldn't, they'd probably just think

I was trying to make up for the business I'd lost when they were shooting out in front on Thursday and Friday, despite the compensation I'd been provided.

Now I had a plan.

I just had to hope it would bear fruit.

CHAPTER 8

Hollywood Confidential

I didn't tell Deanne about my plans, however. She and Mike went to church each Sunday at eleven, and I didn't want to disrupt their routine by asking her to come in to work just because I'd gotten a wild hair. Also, while I adored my friend and knew she would do anything for me, I could never be sure whether she would be able to keep her mouth shut at a critical juncture, and this was the sort of operation that required some delicacy.

So, I was flying solo.

Because no one had expected the coffee shop to be open, it wasn't as though there would be a bunch of customers beating down the door to come in and get a shot of much-needed caffeine. However, I had two small metal bistro sets I arranged out front whenever the weather was fine, and I figured setting them up and putting a sandwich board with the morning's offerings out front would be enough to advertise that Levitation Latte was open for business.

I'd come in around seven and started baking, and by ten o'clock, I had enough muffins and pastries ready to go that I figured it was safe to open. The shop's regular hours were seven to three-thirty, but since it was a Sunday and not when I'd usually be open for business anyway, I had a feeling the late start wouldn't be too much of a problem.

In fact, after I'd put out the bistro tables and the sandwich board, a good ten or fifteen minutes ticked past before anyone showed up at all.

Unfortunately, my first customer of the day wasn't one of the *Perdition Row* cast and crew, as I'd hoped, but Kyle Isaacs.

He was wearing his Las Vegas P.D. uniform, so I knew he must be on duty. Most likely, he'd been cruising down Bridge Street, had noticed the coffee shop was open when it shouldn't be, and had decided to swing by and see what was going on.

"You're open," he said as he approached the counter.

A completely unnecessary remark, but one he probably had decided he needed to make as a way to open the conversation.

"Yep," I said, trying my best to sound cheerful and completely guileless. "I got bored being closed four days in a row, so I thought I'd come in for a short day. Want a muffin?"

As I'd hoped, deflecting him toward perusing the offerings in the bakery case seemed to have staved off any further questioning. He bent down to take a look, hazel eyes narrowing slightly. "I'll try one of those new walnut spice ones. And a latte, please."

"Coming right up," I said, and headed over to the Breville to get the brew going. Just as I was about to bend down and retrieve the muffin he'd requested, Kyle spoke again.

"You heard about Max?"

His tone was way too casual. Despite that, I thought I noted a glint of eagerness in his eyes. He was probably hoping I'd remained blissfully ignorant about the crime, and so he'd have the opportunity to be the one to provide all the gory details.

"Deanne told me," I said, which was only the truth.

Kyle didn't quite deflate, but I could tell he was disappointed he wouldn't get to be the person to spill all the gory details. "Oh, right," he replied. "Crazy thing, isn't it?"

You have no idea, I thought. *And Max being suspected of murder isn't the half of it.*

Of course, I knew better than to tell Kyle that I'd talked to the suspect, had actually tried to do a tea-leaf reading to unearth the real perpetrator.

Not that there was anything illegal about talking to Max, since it wasn't as though he'd been locked up or even formally charged.

Yet.

But I knew deep down that Kyle...and, by extension, Chief DeVargas...probably wouldn't be too happy to learn I'd been offering aid and advice to a possible murderer, so I nodded and said, "Totally crazy. Do you really think he's guilty?"

Kyle scratched the back of his head and frowned slightly, pondering my question. "I don't know," he said at last. "I mean, the evidence seems pretty clear-cut, but I didn't see the actual crime scene. I just heard about it from Cody Rivera."

Another officer on the force, a guy about ten years older than we were, and so not as much a part of our little high school network. I didn't know much about Cody, except I guessed he must have been one of the cops who'd responded to the initial call regarding Perry Lockhart's death.

"Oh?" I said as I set Kyle's muffin on a plate and then headed back to pour the espresso I'd just brewed into a pitcher. With any luck, I could draw out the whole latte-making procedure long enough to get the whole story from him.

He reached for the muffin and broke off a piece. Right before he popped it in his mouth, he said, "Yeah, I guess Perry Lockhart's assistant found him Saturday morning. She got worried when he wasn't responding to any of her texts, so she called 9-1-1, and dispatch sent Cody over to his house to take a look."

"Perry wasn't staying at the hotel with everyone else?" I inquired, pouring milk into the pitcher of espresso. Yes, Max had told me something about a vacation rental, but I knew I needed to play dumb and act as though I knew absolutely nothing about the crime.

Kyle's shoulders lifted. "I guess not. He was renting that Airbnb over on Gonzalez Street."

I knew the place—it was an adorable little stone cottage owned by Lorraine Tyler, who also had an antique store only a few doors down from Levitation Latte. Poor Lorraine. Would she now have to let all her guests know that someone had been murdered on the premises?

Fingers crossed Perry hadn't decided to haunt the place. That would be really bad for business.

And it didn't seem too odd to me that the *Perdition Row* director would want to stay someplace where he wouldn't be cheek by jowl with the rest of the crew. The Plaza Hotel had some very nice rooms, but even the choicest suite there wouldn't be as private as staying in his own house. For all I knew, he'd been irritated that Max had leased Sunset Ridge for a month and had tried to copy him by also renting a private place, albeit one considerably less grand.

I stuck the steam wand in the pitcher and kept an eye on the foam level as I prompted, "So... Officer Rivera found him?"

Kyle nodded but didn't speak, since he had a mouth full of muffin at the time. Once he was done chewing, he replied, "Right. He was lying in the middle of the living room floor, and I guess the lights were still on. That's why we're pretty sure he was murdered sometime last night rather than this morning. But we'll have to wait for the M.E. to get back to us on that."

A task I assumed would be handled first thing Monday morning, unless Chief DeVargas had requested that the autopsy be expedited. One would think that in a case with such a high-profile victim, the coroner's office would be on it right away.

Or maybe not. Before I headed over to the coffee shop this morning, I'd taken a quick peek at social media and a few celebrity gossip sites, and I hadn't seen a single word about Perry Lockhart's death. The rumors might have already spread across Las Vegas, but it didn't seem as if anyone had been inclined to talk up the scandal beyond our local grapevine. When something bad affected one of our own, we tended to circle the wagons and hunker down.

And I had to believe that the producers of *Perdition Row* would be doing everything in their power to keep this all under wraps for as long as possible, maybe even threatening the cast and crew with some sort of blacklist if they didn't keep their mouths shut. Once Max was charged with the crime—*if* he was charged, I reminded myself, which seemed like a long shot at this point—then it would be a matter of public record, and I had to assume my quiet little town would soon be swarming with reporters.

For now, though, I'd let myself be glad the outside world was blissfully unaware of the tragedy that had struck the set of Max Sullivan's latest movie.

"Did it look as though there was a struggle?" I asked. A long shot, maybe, and yet there was always the chance they'd just assumed Perry must have been shot with Max's gun because it was the same caliber or something, and instead the *Perdition Row* director had simply been in the wrong place at the wrong time, the victim of a robbery gone bad. I loved my town, but I knew it had some rough edges, and neighborhoods where I wouldn't walk alone after dark. It didn't seem completely implausible that someone had discovered a rich Hollywood director was staying in the Airbnb, someone with a fancy watch or an expensive phone or whatever else might be worth stealing.

However, even as I set his latte down in front of him, Kyle quashed that hope, saying, "No, the place was completely undisturbed. Either he was caught by surprise, or he knew the assailant."

He didn't add, *Which is why we all think it was Max,* but I got the message.

"Well, I hope you figure it out," I said lightly. "But I do have a hard time believing Max could have done something like this."

"It sounds like that director was pretty rough on him."

I lifted an eyebrow. "So? You can't survive in Hollywood and be as successful as Max is without having a thick skin. I kind of doubt a few insults would be enough to set him off."

Honestly, I didn't think there was anything in the world that could compel Max to commit murder. The heroes he played might have been okay with racking up an impressive body count in the pursuit of righteousness, but my friend wasn't that guy. He was much more likely to sit back and allow the wheels of justice to turn, no matter how slowly.

Kyle's face was a study in conflict. I could tell he wanted to contradict me but knew deep down I was only telling the truth. He and Max had never been besties or anything like that, and yet he knew Las Vegas's golden boy well enough to realize he just didn't have that sort of instinct for violence.

So, he drank some latte and was silent for a moment before giving another shrug. "I guess that's for the D.A. to decide." A pause, and then he sent a somewhat guilty glance toward the squad car parked outside and said, "I should probably get going. How much do I owe you?"

We'd had this same exchange so many times that now I could only smile. "It's on the house. Be careful out there."

"Always am."

Latte in one hand—he'd polished off the muffin, with only a few crumbs remaining on the plate—he headed out, the easy saunter of his walk telling me he didn't have a care in the world.

Well, that made one of us.

A few more customers came and went after that, several of them locals who were surprised but happy to see Levitation Latte was open on this unexpected Sunday morning, and the rest obviously members of the *Perdition Road* crew. They all looked a bit shell-shocked, as though they didn't know quite what to do with themselves but had decided an injection of caffeine was just what the doctor ordered.

I sold muffins and bagels and a few ham and cheese croissants, and dispensed lattes and macchiatos and the odd iced coffee. A little after one, there was a bit of a lull, and I poured myself some tea and sneaked a bagel out of the display case, thinking that should be enough to fortify me until I could get home and have something a bit more solid.

And then Lauralee Peters walked in.

Her pale blonde hair was what gave her away, because I had to admit that the red-eyed, drawn woman I saw in front of me now was a far cry from the golden goddess I'd spied emerging from her trailer a few days before. Without even a glance at me, she went and sat down at a table in the corner farthest from the front door, clearly expecting me to come wait on her, even though I had a sign posted that stated customers were supposed to come up to the counter to place their orders.

Well, things were pretty slow right now, and I wanted to talk to her anyway.

I approached the table and did my best to act as though I hadn't noticed the telltale signs of recent weeping in her face. "What can I get you?" I asked.

"How about an Irish coffee?" she replied, her gaze still not meeting mine.

As much as I would have liked to oblige her—she definitely looked like a woman who needed a drink—I knew that wasn't going to happen. "I'm sorry," I said. "I don't have a liquor license."

An exaggerated sigh left her lips, but then she said, "That's all right. Just bring me a coffee with whipped cream. I'll make my own."

And she reached in her bag and pulled out a

silvery flask.

Oh, boy. I supposed I could have told her I couldn't allow her to drink on the premises, since doing so meant risking a fine, but I really wasn't in the mood to argue with a distraught movie star right then. Besides, she'd clearly walked over here from the Plaza Hotel, so it wasn't as though I had to worry about her getting behind the wheel after this.

Without comment, I headed back to the counter and got out the whipping cream from the fridge, then made a small batch to go on top of the cup of coffee I also poured for her. As I walked back over to Lauralee Peters' table, I had to wonder when she'd last indulged herself with something like whipped cream. A long time, I guessed, which only seemed to speak to her current agitated state.

As soon as I put the coffee down on the table in front of her, she unscrewed the flask and dumped enough of the golden liquid into the cup that it nearly overflowed. Even from where I stood, I could smell the sharp scent of brandy.

Okay, not an Irish coffee, then, but her version of a quickie Alexander.

Figuring I wasn't going to get a better opening than this—and also guessing that Lauralee had already partaken of some of the contents of her flask before she ever got here—I ventured, "Um...is everything okay?"

Her reddened eyes moved up toward me. Not hostile, exactly, but almost puzzled, as though she couldn't quite figure out why a peon like me was presuming to ask personal questions of a celebrity. To my relief, though, she didn't tell me to get lost, but instead replied, "I suppose you've heard."

"'Heard'?" I echoed.

Now she looked downright irritated. She lifted her doctored coffee to her lips and said, "About Perry Lockhart."

Immediately, I did my best to assume an expression of somber concern. "Um, yes. It's terrible...and terrible that they think Max Sullivan might have had anything to do with it. I can see why you'd be upset."

Lauralee's expertly groomed brows drew together for a second or two. Then comprehension seemed to dawn, and she gave a bitter chuckle. "Why the hell would you think I cared anything about Max Sullivan?"

Although I'd heard directly from Max that there was absolutely nothing between him and his costar, I still hadn't been able to put all those doubts to bed. "Well, um...." I hedged, then hurriedly added as she sent me an impatient glance, "I suppose I read somewhere that you two were a thing."

Her mouth twisted. Even in her current distressed state, she still hadn't forgotten to put on lipstick—a sheer rose color that went well with her fair skin and blue eyes—before leaving the hotel. Now sounding almost amused, she said, "Honey, don't believe everything you read in the tabloids."

And she took another large swallow of brandy and coffee.

I wanted to protest that I didn't read the tabloids at all, but then I realized I'd probably get Lauralee to reveal more if I continued to pretend I was some naïve, not-too-bright chick from the sticks. "Oh," I said. "Then why...?"

"Why am I so upset?" she finished for me, punctuating the question with a coffee/brandy chaser. "Because," she went on before I could reply, "I wasn't having an affair with Max Sullivan. I was having an affair with Perry Lockhart."

Well, I hadn't seen that one coming. Or at least, I thought that someone as gorgeous and successful as Lauralee Peters could do better than her former director, who had to be at least ten or twelve years older than she and definitely didn't seem like a guy who would provide much in the way of emotional support.

Again, she continued without allowing me to speak. "He was brilliant, positively brilliant. I'd been waiting to work with him for years. As soon as we met, I could feel the sparks between us. This movie was going to be amazing, my chance to rack up some real awards."

The catty part of me wondered if that was the real reason she'd shacked up with Perry, but then I pushed the thought away as uncharitable. Sometimes, the heart did what it wanted to do, and logic got shoved to the side.

Obviously, or I could've told that troublesome organ that my crush on Max was never going to go anywhere and I needed to manage my expectations.

"I'm very sorry," I murmured. However, since I was playing amateur sleuth and knew I shouldn't leave things there, I made myself ask, "But you weren't with Perry at his house?"

She slanted a sideways look up at me through her long lashes, but apparently she'd already drunk enough brandy that she wasn't guarding herself the way she probably would have if sober. Instead of asking me how I knew about Perry's rented Airbnb, she just said, "I was there earlier that evening, but we both decided we needed to be discreet. I went back to my hotel room around nine, and so he was alone when...when it happened."

Tears glittered in her eyes, and she gulped down some more coffee and brandy, this time getting a smear of whipped cream along her upper lip. Either she was an even better actress than I'd thought, or she really had cared about the guy.

But if she was that great an actress, then maybe she could be stringing me along, doing her best to make it seem as though she was the heartbroken girlfriend—or whatever she'd been to Perry Lockhart—and nothing else. If she'd been over at his Airbnb, then she would have had ample opportunity to shoot him.

Exactly why Lauralee Peters would have felt the need to shoot her director/lover point-blank in the chest, I really didn't know. She might have truly cared about him, or maybe not, but an actress dreaming of Oscar gold wouldn't do anything that could destroy those chances, would she?

I didn't think so, but then again, I didn't live in her world. I didn't know what motivated her, what would have driven her to do something so desperate.

A sniff, and she drank some more of her high-octane coffee. "I don't think Max did it, though," she went on. "I mean, he had every reason to... Perry was an utter ass to him...but Max just isn't that kind of guy."

Pretty much the same thought had gone through my own head multiple times ever since hearing the awful news. Still, I had to ask, "You know Max pretty well?"

She shrugged. Up close like this, she seemed almost frail, so slender I could practically break her over my knee...and I wasn't exactly built like a linebacker. "We worked on a couple of movies together. We're friendly." A pause, and the next glance she shot up toward me, while bleary, seemed to also carry with it a certain level of recognition. "You're the mystery woman, aren't you?"

I blinked. "Excuse me?"

Yes, that was definitely a knowing gleam in her bloodshot blue eyes. "I saw you coming out of Max's trailer the other day."

And here I'd thought Lauralee Peters was too lofty a being to notice an ordinary mortal like me... well, unless she needed me to fetch her a coffee or something.

"I dropped by for a quick chat," I said. "We've known each other since we were kids—we grew up as neighbors."

Lauralee gave a knowing nod. "Ah, the girl next door."

The words slipped out, sounding way too hopeful. "He talked about me?"

"Oh, not in so many words," she replied, effectively quashing any hope that Max might have been harboring a secret crush of his own all these years. "But he made a comment once or twice about coming from a small town and still not being totally used to how we do things in Hollywood, and that was why he never seemed to date actresses. His girlfriends might have been in the business— casting agents or makeup artists or whatever—but they worked behind the scenes."

That probably explained why the tabloids

didn't discuss Max's private life as much as one might think, considering his celebrity, and why they'd been so eager to manufacture a relationship between him and Lauralee. I didn't really like the idea of him dating anyone, immature as such a response might have been, but at least he wasn't chasing after a bunch of starlets.

"I'm glad he has a friend here, though," Lauralee went on. She stared down into her cup, now nearly empty.

For a moment or two, I worried that she was going to ask for some more coffee, and whether I'd be able to tell her I didn't feel comfortable getting her another drink. Yes, the one ingredient I was providing was innocent enough…it was what she would do to it afterward that worried me.

But apparently she'd decided she'd needed to stop there, because she shook her head and pushed the cup away.

"How much?" she asked.

"On the house," I said. Not that I thought she couldn't afford the three bucks, but the woman had just suffered a pretty big emotional blow, and I wanted to make the gesture, small as it was.

"Thanks," she replied, and managed a bleary smile. "Yep, I can tell you'd be a good friend." She stopped there for a moment before adding,

"Max is going to need one."

CHAPTER 9

Proof in the Pudding

There was enough of a lull after Lauralee Peters left that I got out my phone and checked it for any messages or texts. Nothing from Max, but a pang of guilt went through me as I realized I really should have been the one reaching out to him. I'd gotten so caught up in getting the shop ready to open and then talking with Kyle and Lauralee that it had completely slipped my mind.

So, I wrote up a quick text, trying to console myself that it was only a little after one, and for all I knew, Max was the type to sleep in late and maybe hadn't even really gotten moving too much yet. Probably a vain hope, one I'd conjured to make myself feel a little less awful about the situation, but there wasn't much I could do about it now except hope he wouldn't be too angry with me.

There've been a couple of developments, I wrote.

How about you come over tonight so we can talk? I'll make you a home-cooked dinner.

And then I sent the message before I could lose my nerve. Was that too much, asking him over for dinner? Yes, there was the excuse that I needed to talk to him, but....

You don't have to cook for me, came back almost at once. *Why don't I take you out?*

At first, I thought that sounded like a great idea. After all, hadn't I always dreamed about the two of us going out on a date? Not that this would be a real date, of course, but still.

Just as quickly, though, reality set in as I realized that going out to eat with Max, considering the current circumstances, probably wasn't the best idea in the world.

It would probably be safer to stay in, I told him. *I don't mind cooking. You know me—the kitchen witch!*

Not that I thought I really fit the standard definition of that term. It wasn't as though I was always brewing up potions and tinctures or whatever, but Mrs. Carmichael swore that my ginger green tea—lightly laced with turmeric—worked better on her arthritis than anything she could take over the counter, while Mr. Salvatore down the street informed me all the time that my peppermint and willow bark brew took care of his migraines faster than the medication his doctor had prescribed. Still, I did enjoy cooking and baking, and making a meal for Max was something I would love to do.

Apparently, he'd also realized that it would be smarter to stay out of the public eye, because he wrote back, *How can I turn down a dinner from a kitchen witch? Sounds like a plan. What time?*

Seven? I replied, which seemed safe enough. Even with getting home from the shop around four, that would give me plenty of time to throw something together.

See you then.

I didn't say, *It's a date.* No, that would have been beyond awful. Instead, I sent back a thumbs-up, signaling we'd locked in the plan and I'd see him that evening.

Now I just had to figure out what to make.

Several more of the *Perdition Row* cast and crew wandered in and out of the coffee shop that afternoon, but, unlike Lauralee Peters, none of them seemed inclined to be chatty. No, they all appeared a little mooney and disoriented, as if none of them really knew what to do next, but getting a caffeine fix felt like the right thing to do.

I got some locals, too, but the place definitely wasn't busy enough to keep me occupied. No, I watched the clock, turned over a bunch of recipes in my mind, doing my best to determine which one was exactly right for the occasion, and then gratefully locked up the shop at three-thirty and prepared to flee.

Not before setting out fresh food and water for Tilly, of course—she'd pretty much decimated what I'd previously left behind for her—and making sure the place was swept, the tables wiped down, so Deanne and I would be ready to hit the ground running the next morning. Still, even after managing all those tasks, I was out the door by three forty-five.

All my ruminations about dinner had brought me to the conclusion that I should make chicken and dumplings. Maybe that was a hopelessly down-home meal for someone like Max, who probably dined at five-star restaurants every night of the week. At the same time, though, I knew he'd enjoyed meals like that back in school when my grandmother would make dinner for him from time to time—Tina Sullivan was a lovely woman, but she definitely didn't enjoy cooking—and so I thought it might be fun to put together something so thoroughly nostalgic.

Luckily, the house was already pretty much spotless...well, except the fourth bedroom, which I used as a combination storage dump and workspace, and Max would have no reason to go in there...so I didn't have to do much except focus on getting dinner ready. As I peeled and chopped and measured, though, I couldn't stop thinking about Lauralee Peters, about her revelation that she and Perry Lockhart had been having an affair. Nothing particularly wrong with that, since they were both apparently unattached adults, but what if someone in the cast or crew had found out about the relationship? Maybe one of Lauralee's cast mates was equally enamored of her, and had shot Perry in a fit of jealous rage.

That actually sounded like a pretty good theory, or it would be, if it weren't for the sticky part about the gun being locked up in a storage unit and basically inaccessible to everyone.

Unless the jealous party turned out to be Jon Hansford, the armorer. He definitely would have had access to the weapon. Possibly, my earlier theory about Jon being in love with Perry would still work in such a scenario. If he'd learned about Perry and Lauralee being together, he might have lost control and decided to get rid of the man who wouldn't return his affections.

All right, I knew there were a bunch of massive assumptions in that scenario, chief among them that I didn't even know whether Jon Hansford was gay. But Max should be able to clear up that question for me.

If nothing else, all the theorizing kept my brain

busy while I worked, and soon enough, seven o'clock rolled around. The house was full of delicious smells, and I'd set two places at the dining room table and put out a bottle of pinot noir that I hoped my dinner guest would find acceptable, even if it had come from the local Walmart. Because I wanted this to feel like a friendly, no-pressure meal, I hadn't lit any candles, or even dimmed the iron chandelier that hung over the table.

No, this was just a couple of friends getting together for dinner and nothing more.

Right.

Max was a few minutes late, but I wouldn't hold that against him, not when I knew his was a life where he had people doing for him all the time, including holding him to a schedule. He'd mentioned an assistant, but I hadn't seen hide nor hair of her...or him, although I got the feeling his assistant was probably a woman. For all I knew, he hadn't even brought her with him to Las Vegas, but had left her behind in L.A. so she could keep things running there while he was working on location.

To my surprise, he was carrying a bouquet of flowers, gorgeous blue and white hydrangeas, a perfect match for my recently renovated house.

"You didn't have to do that," I said when he handed them to me.

"Yes, I did," he replied with a winning smile.

"You're helping me out...and you made me dinner. That at least calls for some flowers."

"Well, they're gorgeous," I told him. "Why don't you go ahead and sit down, and I'll put these in some water."

He nodded and went into the dining room, taking a seat there, although I noticed he chose the chair to the right of the one at the head of the table. I'd expected him to take the place of honor, but it seemed he wanted me to sit there.

I wouldn't comment, though.

Seating arrangements were the least of our problems.

After I fetched one of my grandmother's old milk-glass vases from the cupboard above the fridge and put the hydrangeas in some water, I returned to the dining room and set the impromptu arrangement down on the sideboard. "Dinner will be ready in just a minute," I said. "Why don't you go ahead and open the wine?"

"Sure thing."

I'd left a waiter-style corkscrew sitting on the table next to the bottle of wine, and he picked up both items and got to work. That evening, he was wearing an untucked polo shirt in a shade of blue that almost matched his eyes, along with jeans and boat shoes. Ultra-casual, but then, so was I, since I'd put on a fresh top when I got home but otherwise hadn't bothered to change my daily uniform of jeans and sandals.

Clearly, both of us were trying hard to make this look like anything other than a date.

By the time I got the pot of chicken and dumplings, the basket of cornbread muffins, and bowls of salad and green beans on the table, Max had opened the wine and poured a nice measure of pinot into each of our glasses. With each successive dish I brought out, his eyes had gotten a little wider.

"You're sure you're not inviting the rest of the cast over, too?" he joked as I sat down and spread my napkin in my lap.

I shot him back a grin almost as wide as one of his own. "Well, I thought you should get a proper meal. Lord knows what you've been eating in L.A."

"A lot of sushi," he said, and I couldn't help making a face.

"Sorry, not a fan," I remarked. "I like my food cooked."

"You don't know what you're missing." But he was smiling, and when he raised his glass so I could clink mine against it, he added, "Here's to cooked food."

I could definitely drink to that. After a swallow of pinot, I said, "You seem pretty cheery today."

For just a fraction of a second, his smile looked a little tight. But then he tilted his head, as if to acknowledge that his current demeanor seemed a bit at odds with what was currently going on in his life.

"Well, I talked to Phillip, my lawyer," Max replied. "And he's found someone to take my case. She's flying into Albuquerque tonight, and so she'll be here tomorrow when the charges are filed."

He seemed very calm, all things considered. But then, knowing he had an expert coming to town for both legal and moral support had probably helped to take a little of the edge off.

I almost said, *If the charges are filed,* but then thought better of it. The last thing I wanted was to torture my friend with false hope, especially when he'd made it sound as though there wasn't much chance Chief DeVargas would back off and decide the evidence was too flimsy to pursue the matter.

"'She'?" I echoed.

Max dished some chicken and dumplings for me, and then put about the same amount on his plate. While he was busy, I got a cornbread muffin out of the basket and helped myself to salad and green beans as well. Once he'd added all the extras to his own plate, he responded, "Beverly Cursio. Probably the best criminal defense lawyer in L.A. She's going to check into the Hotel Castañeda after she drives here from Albuquerque."

The Castañeda was a relic leftover from the

Harvey Hotel era, when traveling by train was a romantic adventure with an architecturally interesting hotel staffed by pretty girls in black and white uniforms waiting for you at every stop. It was actually owned by the same people who'd bought and restored the Plaza Hotel, although the Castañeda had only opened a few years ago. It seemed a logical place for Max's lawyer to stay, as it offered amenities you wouldn't find in the town's other lodgings but also offered safe separation between the woman who would be defending him and the cast and crew of *Perdition Row*.

"Good call," I remarked.

I'd caught him as he was taking his first bite of chicken, so I had to wait for him to finish chewing. When he was done, he shot me another of those brilliant Max Sullivan smiles. "Skye, this is incredible."

"Thanks," I said, trying my best to be sound casual, but inside I was doing the happy dance. I kind of doubted any of the women Max had dated in Los Angeles were able to cook like this.

"But yeah," he went on, "Thank God the Castañeda finally opened. I definitely didn't want Beverly staying the same place as the crew, and there aren't any other places in town that felt appropriate for someone who earns a thousand bucks an hour."

My eyes widened. I'd known that top lawyers

made a ton of money, but a thousand bucks an hour?

Clearly, I should have chosen a different vocation.

But no, I didn't really mean that. I loved the coffee shop, loved that I was my own boss and could set my own hours. And because my grandmother had left me the house and my business free and clear, it wasn't as though I had to earn six figures to be comfortable.

Still, I could see that Max had a point. Also, I doubted this Beverly Cursio would be spending much time in Las Vegas—most likely, she'd be here just long enough to offer counsel after he was formally charged, and then whenever they had to come back for the trial.

If there was even a trial at all. I kept hoping the case would get dismissed for lack of evidence, no matter whose fingerprints were on that damn gun.

"You said in your text there were some developments?" Max asked next. He'd been so busy sampling everything on his plate that he hadn't even drunk any wine other than that first sip after our impromptu toast, but now he reached for his glass as he waited for my reply.

I nodded. "Well, I did a tea leaf reading yesterday afternoon, but the only really conclusive shape I could see in the cup was a heart." Pausing there, I did my best to get a good read on his expression. He looked vaguely confused, one friendly brow lifted just a little bit.

"'A heart'?" he repeated. "What's that supposed to signify?"

In this particular case, I had no idea. But I knew I had to try to puzzle my way through it. "Well, generally a heart indicates some kind of romantic relationship. And then after I met Lauralee—"

"You met her?" Max broke in. "When?"

"Earlier today. I thought I'd try opening the coffee shop to see if any of the cast or crew might show up, and if they did, whether I'd be able to get any information out of them. In Lauralee's case, I hit pay dirt." I paused there, then did my best to study my friend's expression without actually looking as though I was watching him closely. As far as I could tell, his features showed interest but nothing else.

Might as well go for it.

"Did you know she was having an affair with Perry Lockhart?"

Still nothing. Maybe a very small lift at the corner of one mouth, but that was it. He could have been acting, doing his best to conceal his feelings from me, and yet I didn't think so.

And when he spoke, his tone was musing, but certainly didn't betray even a flicker of jealousy.

"I had a feeling," he said, then broke off a piece

of cornbread muffin and smeared some butter on it. "I mean, they didn't advertise it or anything. But part of being an actor is studying people's interactions, learning from them, and I noticed the way Perry would touch her arm when no one was looking, or the way they'd exchange what you could only call weighted glances."

Thank God he didn't seem upset by the relationship. No, as far as I could tell, he appeared more amused by it than anything else. Clearly, he didn't have any particular emotional attachment to his co-star.

And that meant I wouldn't have to tiptoe through the next part of our conversation.

"Well, because I saw the heart in my tea leaf reading," I said, "I thought maybe someone murdered Perry out of jealousy...someone who wanted to be with Lauralee, or someone who maybe wanted to be with Perry himself and couldn't stand seeing him with anyone else." I paused there; Max looked thoughtful, but again, I didn't see anything in those friendly, handsome features that would indicate he found our current topic of conversation uncomfortable. Since he didn't seem inclined to say anything, I ventured, "Can you think of anyone like that?"

He took a bite of muffin and then set it down, wiping his fingers on the napkin in his lap before he reached for his wine glass and took a sip. "In

Lauralee's case, I'd say there are probably a ton of people who would have liked to get Perry out of the way once they found out he was in a relationship with her. She has some pretty devoted fans."

Not for the first time, I reflected that riches and fame weren't all they were cracked up to be. The thought of having fans who were so crazy about you that they'd be okay with offing a rival wasn't exactly reassuring. "Anyone in particular stand out?"

Max shook his head, drank some more wine, and then set down his glass. "You'd have to ask Lauralee about that. I heard she has some restraining orders against a few people, but it's not the sort of thing she likes to talk about."

No, that wouldn't be a very comfortable topic of conversation. "I don't know whether she'd confide in me about that sort of thing."

That comment made Max lift an eyebrow as he settled against the back of his chair, wine glass still in hand. "She told you about her affair with Perry."

I managed a lopsided smile. "Well, to be fair, she was kind of drunk at the time."

"Drunk in a coffee shop?"

"She brought a flask."

He chuckled, drank a little more wine, and then straightened so he could set the glass back down and retrieve his fork. "Very resourceful." A few more bites of chicken and dumplings, and he said, "I could try to ask her, but I doubt she wants to talk to me right now, considering I'm the guy accused of murdering her lover."

"Oh, you'd be surprised," I said, and helped myself to a forkful of green beans. "She doesn't think you did it, either."

Now Max looked pleased, as though he'd been secretly worried that his fellow cast members must have been convinced of his guilt. "She doesn't?"

"No," I replied. "And I have to admit it would be kind of nice to blame this whole thing on a crazed fan."

"But how would a crazed fan get his hands on that gun?"

Good question. I certainly didn't have any answers right now, and unless the tea leaves started giving me some truly actionable information, I didn't have any idea how I would even begin to find those much-needed clues. "I don't know," I said. Sitting here with Max, my theory about Jon Hansford the armorer was feeling more and more outlandish, but I told myself I might as well ask. "What if the jealousy was directed toward Perry, not Lauralee? Someone who knew him well and had been harboring a secret crush all this time?"

God, it felt so awkward asking that question, considering those words could have easily been used to describe me. At least, as Lauralee had said, Max had always been pretty circumspect when it came to his love life, and so I'd never had to suffer an awkward flare of jealousy when reading about his romantic exploits in the tabloids.

Not that I would ever feel compelled to pick up a gun and attempt to rectify the situation.

To say Max looked skeptical after I asked my question would have been an understatement. He set his fork down on his plate, expression wry. "Somehow, I just don't see Perry as the object of someone's unrequited passion."

Neither did I, but stranger things had been known to happen. "Well, he hooked up with Lauralee, so...."

"Point taken."

Because I'd already gone out on a limb, I figured I might as well ask the question that had been bobbing around in the back of my mind for a good chunk of the day. "Do you think it might have been Jon?"

Max blinked at me, his brain obviously having a difficult time processing that bewildering query. After a moment, he said, "What...Jon Hansford, the armorer?"

"Yes," I replied. "You mentioned the other day that he and Perry have worked together a lot."

Once again, Max seemed to retreat into befuddled silence. Then he chuckled and said, "I suppose that would make it easy, wouldn't it? I mean, the guy had plenty of access to all the weapons we were using on set. Problem is, I've worked with Jon, too, and so I happen to know he's been happily married for almost twenty-five years and just sent his oldest daughter off to Stanford. I suppose there's just the remotest chance he's been closeted all this time, but I somehow doubt it."

Well, there went that theory. Holding back a sigh, I reached for my wine glass and took a larger-than-normal swallow.

"Then I guess we're back to square one."

Max, however, wasn't so easily deflated. His mouth lifted in an encouraging smile, and he said, "I think we're a little farther along than that. Your tea leaves are suggesting that there's some sort of romantic angle involved in Perry's murder. We just have to figure out what it is."

All right, maybe that narrowed things down just the teeniest little bit. I drank some more wine, then responded, "And if we don't?"

My friend's smile didn't waver in the slightest. Still with that sunny glint in his blue eyes, he said, "Then I guess I'll get to find out how good an attorney Beverly Cursio really is."

CHAPTER 10

Over–Charged

Max didn't stay late; despite his outwardly relaxed appearance, I got the impression he was getting more and more on edge as time ticked past and Monday got closer and closer.

Monday, when the D.A. was supposed to formally charge him with murder and he'd be arraigned. Not for the first time, I wondered why they hadn't done so immediately and just gotten it over with.

But Max Sullivan wasn't exactly your garden-variety murder suspect, and with a face that would be recognized almost anywhere he went, it wasn't as though Chief DeVargas could have worried he was much of a flight risk. No, the chief had probably decided it was better to let the D.A. work on the case over the weekend so he'd have something iron-clad to present to the judge on Monday morning.

Well, I didn't care how iron-clad the district attorney thought his case was. I knew he was barking up entirely the wrong tree, and I was going to do my damnedest to discover who'd really pulled that trigger and left Perry Lockhart bleeding out in the living room of his rented house.

No kiss goodnight from Max, of course, but he did surprise me by giving me a quick pat on the shoulder before he thanked me for dinner and headed out. He also promised to text me when he had some news.

"You'd better," I said. "I don't care if I'm in the middle of the morning rush. Just text me, and I'll head right over to the courthouse."

I could make such a promise because I knew Deanne would cover for me in such an eventuality. Also, since Las Vegas was the San Miguel County seat, the courthouse was only a few blocks away. I could drop everything and be there in a couple of minutes.

Max didn't protest, only thanked me again for all my support, then headed down the porch steps and walked over to his rented Bronco. As he went, I thought he must be enjoying the peace and quiet that staying here in his hometown had to offer. From what I'd be able to tell, he was pretty much hounded by paparazzi no matter where he went in

Southern California, but it appeared those rapacious photographers weren't quite as thick on the ground in this part of New Mexico.

Sadly, I knew the peace and quiet wouldn't last, that as soon as news got out about Perry Lockhart's death and Max being formally charged with the crime, the metaphorical poop was going to hit the fan full force.

I closed the door behind him and then locked it. Once upon a time, my grandmother had left the house unlocked unless she was going to be gone for the day, but Las Vegas had suffered its own changes over the years, just like the rest of the world.

Max had helped me clear the table, but I still had a pile of dishes on the counter and pots and pans in the sink. Getting everything cleaned up was going to take a while.

Which was okay. That kind of mindless work would allow me to think—and at least I'd had a dishwasher installed when the kitchen was remodeled, or I would have been looking at even more scrubbing than currently awaited me.

I was wearing a sleeveless top, so I didn't have to worry about rolling up my cuffs to get them out of harm's way. With the warm water flowing, I set to work as I stared out the window into the backyard, now completely dark except for the solar lights that marked the various pathways.

Okay, so I could scratch Jon Bransford off my

list. That still left Letty Mendoza, admittedly a long shot, since she didn't seem to have any kind of history with Perry Lockhart, and...despite his relationship with Lauralee Peters...he didn't seem like the kind of person to inspire the sort of ferocious passion that would drive someone to murder.

And while I supposed Letty could have developed a mad crush on Lauralee, that scenario also seemed pretty implausible.

Which meant I basically had nothing to go on other than the tea leaves' enigmatic message that this was definitely a crime of the heart.

I got the dishes done, and briefly pondered whether I should brew up another batch of tea and see whether this time around I might get a piece of more actionable information. Unfortunately, it was nearing ten o'clock, and I had to be up no later than five. Yes, I could try one of my herbal blends rather than green tea and avoid any caffeine, but I'd still be awake way past my bedtime.

Besides, even if the leaves provided some kind of miraculous revelation, there probably wasn't much I could do about it this late on a Sunday night.

So, I did the practical thing. I wiped down the granite counters, hung up the damp towel, and made myself go to bed. Whatever might happen the next day, I'd just have to deal with it then.

The alarm went off way too early, in a black morning that didn't do much to make me feel better about crawling out of bed at that hour. However, I was used to the schedule, and I told myself it could have been worse. I'd washed my hair the day before, which meant all I needed to do this morning was run a comb through it, spritz it with some water to turn my early morning frizz back into somewhat acceptable waves, and call it a day.

I made myself coffee, though, strong and black, since I was feeling just a little morning-afterish that day, thanks to the bottle of wine I'd shared with Max the night before. It wasn't that I was a complete teetotaler, but in general, I usually only had a single glass with dinner, and often skipped alcohol altogether if I wasn't in the mood. A leftover cornbread muffin generously smeared with butter seemed a quick and easy breakfast, and by five forty-five, I was out the door and headed over to Levitation Latte.

No missed calls or texts, which was about what I'd expected. Max had probably gone straight to bed after he left my place, and it was way too early for him to be up now, even if he did have a possible arraignment hanging over his head. I really hoped he'd gotten a decent night's sleep despite everything.

He deserved it.

Because I'd tidied up before I left the previous afternoon, I went straight to work baking up that morning's batch of muffins, along with some croissants and bagels. By the time Deanne appeared at six-thirty, the whole shop smelled deliciously of baking bread and cinnamon and blueberries, and she inhaled deeply as she pulled on her apron and tied it behind her back.

"I don't think I'll ever get tired of that smell," she said, then pulled in another aromatic breath. "It's a pretty good reward for getting up this early."

"Agreed," I replied. The one cup of coffee I'd had with my cornbread muffin hadn't felt sufficient that morning, and so I already had a pot brewing. "Coffee?"

"Love it."

I poured a cup for both of us, then headed over to the fridge so I could put some cream in mine. After I returned the cream to its shelf and shut the door, I turned back toward Deanne, who now wore a halfway speculative expression.

"I heard you were open yesterday," she said, her tone almost but not quite accusing.

Since I'd known there was no way to keep that particular fact from her, not when I'd had quite a few locals wandering in and out the previous afternoon, I just shrugged. "I thought it might be a good way to gather some intelligence."

Deanne absorbed this explanation, then nodded. "And did you?"

"A little," I said. "I found out Perry Lockhart and Lauralee Peters had some kind of a relationship. But I don't think it had anything to do with his murder."

Although a startled light had entered Deanne's eyes at that particular piece of news, she didn't ask any questions. That was a relief, because she tended to be more uptight about some things than I was, and I had to guess she wouldn't be too thrilled at the news that Ms. Peters had been pouring brandy into her coffee and that I hadn't done anything to stop her. That sort of thing could technically get us in trouble with the restaurant licensing board, and definitely wasn't the sort of mess I wanted to have stirred up right now.

"And Max?" Deanne said next.

"I had him over for dinner last night, and we discussed some possibilities. But neither of us was able to come to any useful conclusions."

Being Deanne, she ignored Max's looming criminal case and instead went straight to the much more important revelation about his having dinner at my house. "He came over?" she demanded. "How did it go?"

"Fine," I said. Clearly, she was thinking that now Max was back in town, we could make up for the decade we'd lost, and he'd finally figure out that the two of us were meant to be together. "I mean, it was friendly, like the past ten years might never have happened. But that's all it was. Just friends."

For a second or two, I wondered if I should tell her about how he'd touched me on the shoulder as he told me goodnight. Then I decided that was probably a bad idea. She'd read way too much into what had only been a gesture of friendship and thanks, and nothing more. All right, maybe even that off-hand touch had been enough to send a little thrill of warmth through my entire body, but luckily, I'd managed to keep it cool. Max hadn't noticed anything.

I hoped.

"Still," Deanne said, clearly unwilling to let it go, "he came over, instead of just hiding out at the ranch. I think that's kind of a big deal."

"He probably wanted to get out and about while he still could," I remarked. "Once he's charged and arraigned, he's going to have a lot less leeway to come and go as he pleases."

Deanne's eyes widened. "You really think it's going to come to that?"

"Unless Chief DeVargas and the D.A. back off, which I kind of doubt is going to happen." Sheer force of will kept me from pulling my phone out of my pocket and taking another look to make sure I hadn't missed any calls or texts while I was getting the muffins ready. It wouldn't be seven o'clock for another twenty minutes, and I highly doubted Max was even awake yet.

The timer on the oven went off, and so I hurried back into the kitchen to pull out the muffins. Deanne came along with me, a frown tugging at her brows. But then her expression cleared, and she actually smiled.

"Well, if Max posts bail but has to stay here, that's good, isn't it?"

By her logic, yes, I supposed that was one way to look at the situation. If the judge told him he had to stay in San Miguel County, then by necessity, we'd probably get to spend a lot more time together doing our best to determine the true culprit before the case actually went to trial.

"Maybe," I allowed. "And we don't even know whether the judge is going to make that a condition of bail or not. Max might just have to stay in the country, which means he'd still be free to go back home to L.A. until it was time to come here for the court case."

Deanne's expression clouded for a moment, but because my friend was the sort of person who could find the silver lining in just about any situation, her smile returned full force. "Oh, I think the judge will want him to stay. Honestly, you'd think Max would want to stick around town anyway. He has family and friends here, and I have to believe it would be a lot easier to dodge paparazzi in Las Vegas."

Which was pretty much what I'd been thinking as well, but I didn't know whether Max would share our view of the situation. I had no clear idea what his house in L.A. was like, because he was pretty strict about maintaining his privacy and never seemed to allow reporters there for interviews, but I imagined it must be some kind of gated compound in Bel-Air or maybe the Hollywood Hills, the sort of place where he could hole up for an extended period, especially if he had an assistant to fetch and carry for him. Sunset Ridge Ranch was gated as well, but the fences surrounding the property weren't that high. A determined paparazzo could easily scale them and then lurk in the shrubbery, just waiting for the moment when Max came out to sit on the patio and drink his morning coffee, or whatever.

In the end, he'd have to do whatever the judge told him to do. His own personal wishes wouldn't have too much weight in the matter, unfortunately.

I said, "I guess we'll just have to see," and Deanne took the hint for what it was. We could do all the speculating in the world, and yet it wouldn't matter one bit in the end. Like Max, we'd just have to wait and see what happened.

And then it was seven o'clock, and we had the usual rush of early morning customers coming in to get their lattes or mocha javas, or Darjeeling or green tea, and there wasn't much chance to talk further. A few people sent me speculative looks, as though they wanted to ask questions about Max, but I did my best to stay bright and cheery, putting up an impenetrable wall of brisk friendliness, and managed to avoid getting the third degree.

Things calmed down a bit around nine, but I wasn't granted much of a reprieve, because at nine-fifteen, the text came in.

At the courthouse at ten.

That was all, but it was enough. All my hoping and wishing hadn't done a darn thing.

Max Sullivan was going to be arraigned in less than an hour.

Deanne told me that of course she'd watch the shop for as long as was necessary, and so I headed over to the courthouse a little before ten. When I'd gotten dressed that morning, I'd put on one of my better pairs of jeans and an actual blouse rather than my usual T-shirt, just in case I had to show up at the courthouse after all. My apron had spared the outfit from getting too messed up during my muffin-making that morning, and a quick dust to get off the rest of the flour had done the trick to make me look mostly presentable.

All the same, I found myself reaching up to self-consciously smooth my hair as I approached the building. It was a spare-looking place in the ubiquitous pueblo style so prevalent throughout northern New Mexico, although with a couple of columns and a shallow set of steps added to the façade as a nod toward more traditional courthouse design.

To my dismay, there were a bunch of people with cameras already clustered there. Clearly, they'd found out about Max's arraignment somehow. Maybe the docket had been made public earlier that morning, and it had set off some kind of Google alert or something. Not being a paparazzo, I couldn't say how it all worked.

A Lincoln Town Car pulled up in front of the courthouse and Max emerged, accompanied by an efficient-looking woman with an impeccable blonde bob. She wore a dark suit and carried a briefcase, so I guessed she must be none other than Beverly Cursio, his thousand-dollar-an-hour attorney.

Immediately, the paparazzi descended, calling out Max's name, peppering him with questions. He didn't look to either side but continued into the building, his lawyer acting as something of a human shield to get him through the mob and safely inside the courthouse.

Watching all this, my first instinct was to leap

into the fray and do my best to keep the horde of photographers away from my friend, but common sense asserted itself. It wouldn't be very smart to identify myself as someone close to Max, someone they might end up hounding in order to get some inside information about his case. Maybe they'd find out about our connection eventually, but I might as well put off that evil day for as long as possible.

Doing my best to look completely casual, I approached the courthouse steps. At once, the paparazzi turned toward me...and then, realizing I was nobody, they started scanning the street to see if anyone more important might be coming along.

I didn't exactly breathe a sigh of relief, but I did feel a lot better once I'd slipped inside the building and taken a seat in the courtroom designated for Max's arraignment. There were only a few places available on a bench in the very back, and so I wouldn't be able to get a decent view of what was going on.

Well, it was better than nothing. At least I was here to lend moral support, even if he probably didn't realize I was in the same room with him.

"All rise," the bailiff intoned, and I dutifully stood with the rest of the spectators. Across the aisle, I glimpsed a flash of too-bright blonde hair that looked halfway familiar, and my eyes narrowed.

Raylene Evans.

She hadn't spotted me, luckily, and I made sure to sit down as quickly as possible once the judge entered the courtroom and the bailiff told everyone to take their seats.

What the heck was Raylene Evans doing here? If nothing else, with a five-, a seven-, and an eight-year-old still at home, you'd think she would have something better to do with her time.

But I remembered how Max had told me about her apparently undying love for him, and how she'd desperately wanted to get back together. That sort of devotion had probably compelled her to do whatever it took to make sure someone was watching her kids so she'd be free to come to the courthouse. I doubted anyone would question her behavior too closely, considering the two of them had been high school sweethearts. It was only natural that she'd want to be here to see what was happening firsthand.

Because I was at the rear of the room, I couldn't hear everything of what was exchanged between the D.A.—a lean, intense-looking man whose cold gaze didn't bode well for my friend's future—and Beverly Cursio. They went back-and-forth for about fifteen minutes or so, with the district attorney presenting the preliminary evidence and Ms. Cursio doing her best to shoot it down.

At length, though, the judge said—clearly enough that even I could hear him, "I rule there's sufficient evidence to proceed to a trial. Mr. Sullivan, if you would please stand."

As murmurs rustled through the courtroom, Max got to his feet. He was wearing a gorgeously tailored gray suit and a dark blue tie, and he held his head high. "Yes, your Honor?"

"Bail is set at one million dollars." The judge paused there; he was an older man with only a fringe of hair around his ears, but his eyes held something that almost looked like a glint of amusement. "I assume you can afford that," he added dryly.

"Yes, your Honor," Max replied. He didn't sound particularly tense; maybe he actually felt better now the moment had arrived and he could start to formulate a game plan for what might come next.

"Well, then." The judge stopped again, eyeing Max and his attorney, gaze flicking over to the district attorney for just a second. "You will remain here in Las Vegas, Mr. Sullivan. If you need to leave San Miguel County for any reason, your attorney must petition the court for your right to do so. Do you understand?"

"Yes, your Honor."

Max's voice didn't shake a bit. Was he secretly glad he could stay put, wouldn't have to go back to

Los Angeles and face all the questions and the inevitable shunning by people he regarded as his peers?

Possibly...or possibly he was acting now as well, putting on a brave front. I couldn't see his face from where I sat, and so I had no idea what expression he was wearing just then.

After that, the D.A. and Max's attorney approached the bench and held a brief convo. Once they were done and had backed away, the judge announced, "The trial will begin on Monday, October third."

Only three weeks away. I tried to console myself that three weeks was plenty of time to clear Max's name and make sure the actual murderer was safely locked up, but considering how much success I'd had so far in that pursuit, I didn't know how hopeful I could be.

It's better than next week, I told myself, which was only the truth.

After that, the bailiff escorted Max away from the bench, probably taking him off to handle his bail payment. I wondered how he'd manage such a thing. Not actually affording it, as the judge had commented; to a guy who regularly made eight figures for a film, a million-dollar bail was basically lunch money. Still, it wasn't the sort of transaction you could put on a credit card. Maybe they'd do a wire transfer or something.

Either way, it looked as though he was going to be tied up in paperwork for the next little while, so I stood, slung my purse over one shoulder, and slipped out while the spectators in the courtroom were still murmuring amongst themselves. I had to assume a bailiff would clear the space soon enough, but there wasn't any point in me sticking around to see what happened next.

Max had been formally charged with Perry Lockhart's murder...and now the real work would begin.

CHAPTER 11

Loose Lips

As I'd expected, Deanne was concerned to hear that Max had been arraigned...but also just a wee bit glad that he would be staying put for the time being. "I knew the judge wouldn't let him go back to L.A.," she said. When I didn't respond right away, but only kept doing my quick tally of the pastries and bagels still left in the bakery case, she added, "What did he say to you?"

"Nothing," I said shortly as I stood up. It looked as though what we had on hand should last through the end of the day, and so I wouldn't have to bake an emergency muffin batch to keep us going until closing. "I had to sit in the back of the courthouse, so I don't think he even knew I was there."

I actually hated the idea of not being able to see him, of Max thinking I'd bailed during his hour of need. Maybe I should have braved the paparazzi and gone up to him when his attorney was escorting him into the courthouse.

But if I'd done that, then they would have marked me as someone worth following. True, they'd probably get bored watching me make lattes all day, but I couldn't count on that. Better to stay anonymous for as long as possible.

My phone chimed then, and I dug it out of my apron pocket.

Max.

I saw you leaving the courtroom, his message said. *Beverly's hiring security for the ranch and says I should stay here as much as possible. Come over tonight for BBQ?*

He wasn't mad at me. He'd known I was there. I wanted to hug the phone, but with Deanne standing there a few feet away, I thought I'd better at least attempt to maintain my cool. Yes, she knew exactly how I felt about Max, and yet I still figured it was smarter to keep my excitement in check.

Sure, I sent back. *Need me to bring anything?*

I was hoping for some of your grandmother's awesome cowboy beans.

That I could do. Or rather, I could manage it if I ducked out of the coffee shop for a bit so I could start the beans in my Instant Pot and then transfer them to a crockpot for the rest of the slow-cooking process.

I can do that, I replied. *Come over around seven?*

Or earlier, if you can. That way, I can send Beverly back to the hotel and give her a break. She's already going at it with my defense.

Which she should be, considering what was at stake. Still, I was just fine with riding to Max's rescue, pot full of cowboy beans in hand.

I'll try, I wrote back. *Hang in there!*

He sent me a smiley face in response, putting a cheerful little period on our convo.

I slipped the phone back into my pocket and looked up to see Deanne watching me, expression inquiring.

Since I didn't see the point in hiding the exchange from her, I nodded. "He wants me to come over to the ranch tonight. Do you think you can watch the shop for about a half hour while I get some beans together?"

"Absolutely. It's going to be quiet until closing anyway."

True enough—we were past the lunch rush, and while we always got a few people coming in for an afternoon pick-me-up, I doubted the foot traffic would be anything Deanne couldn't handle. I thanked her and hurried out back, then got in my car and drove over to the house.

I'd made the beans so many times that I had the recipe memorized. What took the longest was the initial cook of the beans, since I had to wait for the

Instant Pot to gain pressure, actually cook the pintos I'd popped inside, and then wait again for it to depressurize so I could dump them into the crockpot along with the ingredients I'd already assembled. Still, the whole procedure only took a little longer than the half hour I'd promised Deanne, and I rushed back to the shop as soon as the lid was on the crock.

It turned out I hadn't missed much—the place was absolutely empty when I entered through the back room, refastening my apron around my waist as I went.

"A couple of the movie people came in," Deanne informed me as she sipped from an iced coffee she'd made for herself in my absence. "One of them told me they're all going to be heading back to California now that Max has been arraigned."

I should have known the *Perdition Row* cast and crew wouldn't have any reason to stick around, and yet the news sent a little shrill of alarm through me. "What about the movie? They're not going to find a replacement director?"

Deanne pulled some iced coffee through her drink's straw. "I guess not. It sounds like they're going to get paid, though—something about a completion bond, or whatever."

Right. I didn't pretend to know much about the inner workings of film production, but even I knew there usually had to be some kind of insurance to cover the cost of making the movie in case it didn't get finished, for whatever reason. And since this had definitely sounded like a pet project for Perry, there probably wasn't anyone else who wanted to pick up the reins.

Still, I didn't like the idea of everyone associated with the film packing up and scattering to the four winds. What if the tea leaves suddenly decided to provide a clue about one of the crew members, and they were all the way back in California? That distance would make it a lot harder to pick their brains.

Since there didn't seem to be much I could do about the situation, I just had to hope none of them was the real killer. If I did a reading that seemed to directly point to one of them, well, I'd just jump on a plane to L.A. if necessary. It wasn't as though I had a judge's orders keeping me here.

Unlike Max.

"That's good to know," I said. "This whole situation would be even worse if a bunch of innocent bystanders got cheated out of a paycheck."

Even if one of them turned out to be the guilty party, that was no reason for the entire cast and crew to get penalized.

Deanne nodded. "That's what I was thinking." She stopped there, and her expression turned almost sly. "So...you and Max at the ranch tonight, huh?"

"He's going to barbecue," I said. "I'm sure he just wants someone around to help take his mind off what happened today. Nothing's going to happen."

Her mouth pursed, but it seemed she knew better than to tease me in earnest. No, she just gave a sympathetic nod and said, "Tell Max we're all pulling for him."

"I will," I promised.

It seemed that no matter what, Max Sullivan would always be Las Vegas's golden boy.

Well, for some people, anyway. Kyle Isaacs came in right before closing, and although I couldn't say he was exactly gloating, I got the distinct impression he was one of the few who wouldn't exactly be heartbroken if Max was found guilty of Perry Lockhart's murder.

"I suppose you heard what happened today," Kyle said as I slid a banana nut muffin and a latte across the counter toward him.

"How could I not?" I returned, although I decided it was better to keep my mouth shut about how I'd been in the courtroom during the arraignment. I hadn't seen him anywhere around, and guessed he must have been out on patrol. "But that was just the arraignment. It's not like Max has been convicted and sentenced."

Kyle didn't seem too worried by that all-important distinction. "Yet," he said, and took a bite of banana nut muffin.

The confidence in his tone made a tingle of unease pass over me. "What do you mean, 'yet'?" I demanded.

He darted a quick look around, but Deanne was on the other side of the room, wiping down a table where a couple of high school kids had decided to spill most of a mochaccino. "Well, I guess the D.A.'s office has Mr. Lockhart's computer and is going through it to find corroborating evidence to prove he had a troubled relationship with Max. They're also checking all his personal notes and correspondence. Sounds like they're on to something."

I wasn't so sure about that. To me, it seemed more like they were just doing their due diligence.

All I did was shrug, though. If I got too impassioned in my defense of Max Sullivan, then Kyle might start wondering why I had such a vested interest in his innocence. Yes, Max was an old friend, but there were friends, and then there were *friends.*

"Do you think you'll hear anything if they do find something?" I asked next, doing my best to sound merely curious and not as though I had an ulterior motive. One good thing about Kyle—he was way chattier than he should be, and far too likely to let drop important pieces of information about an investigation in an attempt to impress me.

"Oh, probably," he replied, blissfully unaware of the way I was trying to lead him along. "I'm good friends with Patty Josephs—she's a legal assistant in the D.A.'s office."

I didn't know Patty too well, but she occasionally stopped in for coffee and a muffin, even though I couldn't really count her as a Levitation Latte regular. She'd been two years behind us in school, pretty and outgoing. For all I knew, she had kind of a crush on Kyle, and therefore would be more likely to tell him things better kept to herself.

All of which could definitely work to my advantage...if I played my cards right.

"Right," I said, then did my best to emulate Max by flashing Kyle a sunny smile. "It's always good to have friends in high places."

The smile seemed to have had an effect on him, because the tips of Kyle's ears turned bright red. His gaze dropped from mine, and he mumbled, "I'll let you know if I hear anything."

Then he took his coffee and half-eaten muffin, and hurried out of the shop.

Watching him go, Deanne shook her head. "You should go easy on that poor boy."

I didn't bother to point out that Kyle was a year older than we were. However, I probably should have realized that smiling at him in such a way hadn't been very smart. "I guess I wasn't thinking," I said. "But if I can get any inside information out of him, then it might help me figure out who's really responsible for Perry Lockhart's death."

"Won't that compromise the case?" she asked, now looking doubtful.

"Not if I don't say anything to Max," I replied. That sounded about right...or at least, I hoped I was right. "I'd just be using that information for my own investigation. Frankly, I think it's probably better for him to stay put on that ranch and not give anyone else any reason to believe he's doing anything besides getting his defense ready and waiting for the trial to begin."

"Oh, right." Deanne still appeared a little dubious, but that might have been because she really didn't know much more about the judicial system than I did. I knew she'd never been one for police procedurals, was much more into romantic comedies or earnest dramas like *This Is Us*. "Well, as long as you're careful."

"Don't worry," I told her as I went over to turn around the "open" sign in the window and lock up the front door. Three-thirty had just arrived, and I wanted to be out of there as quickly as possible.

It might not have been the precise truth, but I said it anyway.

"I'm always careful."

The beans were done to perfection a little past six-thirty, so I lifted the crock out of its metal housing and set it in the quilted carry case my grandmother had made for it years before. Maybe there were newer and fancier crockpots on the market, but I knew I'd hang on to this one until it died in harness.

When I pulled up to the entrance of Sunset Ridge Ranch, I noticed right away that the gate was closed, rather than standing open the way it had been during my last visit. More importantly, a big, burly individual in a black polo shirt was standing there, keeping watch.

I pushed the button to roll down my window as I came to a stop by the guy, who had to be one of Max's newly hired security guards.

"Your business?" he asked. His tone was pleasant enough, but I couldn't miss the holstered gun that hung at his waist.

Clearly, these guys weren't playing around. Even though I was here on perfectly legitimate business, I couldn't quite hold back the tremor in my voice as I said, "I'm Skye O'Malley. I'm a friend of Max's—he invited me over for dinner."

To my surprise, the guy actually cracked a smile. "Evening, Ms. O'Malley. He's expecting you —go right up."

He reached in his pocket, probably to activate the controls for the gate, because it began to slowly swing open a few seconds later. A small sigh of relief escaping my lips, I pushed the button to roll the window back up and then started to drive down the curving lane that led to the ranch house itself.

It was a long, sprawling building that occupied most of the ridge that gave the ranch its name, creamy white stucco with a sharply pitched roof built to withstand our often snowy winters. The land itself was much more lush than one might have expected, since a creek wound through the ranch's hundred-plus acres, and cottonwoods and elms and sycamores shaded the house.

All in all, it was exactly the sort of tranquil spot one might want to use as a sanctuary while hiding out from the paparazzi.

I didn't see Max's rented Bronco, but I assumed it must be tucked somewhere inside the three-car garage. Figuring he wasn't going anywhere, I pulled up in front of the bay nearest the house, then shut off my Subaru's engine and got out. A minute later,

I had the crockpot in its quilted carry bag in one hand and was heading up to the front door, which was shaded by a small portico.

Before I even had a chance to reach out with my free hand and ring the bell, the door opened, and Max smiled out at me. He was wearing a ridiculous apron emblazoned with a skull and crossbones and the legend "Captain Cook—Surrender Your Buns" printed on it, and he looked as though he didn't have a care in the world.

"Hey, there," he said. "Come on in."

Because I'd been here before, I did my best not to gawk at my surroundings, at the steeply arched ceilings with their accent beams, or the casual but obviously extremely expensive furnishings. "How did you know I was at the door?" I asked as I followed him back to the kitchen, which was roughly three times the size of mine, with gleaming stainless appliances that matched its oversized scale.

"Lou called up to the house to let me know you were on your way," Max replied. He took the quilted carry bag from me. "Anything I need to do with this?"

"Just put it in the oven at around 250 to keep it warm." That was one thing I loved about my inherited crockpot; the ceramic insert looked pretty on a table, but it could also go safely in an oven as long as you didn't crank up the temperature too high. I asked, "Lou's the guy at the gate?"

"Yep." Max went over to the monstrous Wolf oven and turned it on, then opened the door and slid the crock inside. "Beverly hired me a whole set of security. Lou's watching the gate, but I have two other guys walking the perimeter. They'll switch out with another team at midnight."

I wondered where she'd gotten the security team. Lou hadn't looked familiar, and I guessed she must have hired the men from a company down in Albuquerque. Las Vegas, New Mexico, wasn't exactly the kind of place where you could scare up a team of highly trained security professionals at the drop of a hat.

"So...this is serious."

Max turned away from the oven and gave me a nod, but he still didn't look too concerned. "Oh, yeah. Even as we were driving back from the court-house, a bunch of paparazzi were following us. As soon as we crossed onto the property, they made a show of stopping, since they would have been tres-passing if they'd kept following the car, but the security cameras picked them up snooping around the back forty, trying to see if they could come in that way."

Because of course the place had security cameras. I hadn't noticed any on the way in, but I hadn't been looking for them, either. It seemed there were more reasons why Max had rented this place than simply because it was big and luxurious and an easy enough drive into town.

In a way, that made me feel better. Surrounded by security cameras and guards, he had to be safe out here.

However, Max only shrugged in response to my comment on the subject. "Beverly thinks so. I mean, the paparazzi have been a part of my life for years, but now they smell blood in the water, so they're getting extra bold." He stopped there and asked in a much different tone, "Glass of wine?"

I didn't even stop to think. "Love one."

A bottle of chardonnay was sitting in a silvery wine cooler on the granite countertop. He got a couple of glasses from one of the cupboards and poured us each some wine. As he handed the glass to me, he said, "Thanks for coming out here. I'm just...."

He stopped there, as if he wasn't quite sure what he had been trying to say, and I ventured, "Just trying to act normal?"

My suggestion made him relax into a half smile. "Yes, exactly that. Not the easiest thing to do with armed guards prowling the grounds, but I'm trying to roll with it."

I lifted my glass, and he clinked his against it. "Well, here's to normal," I said.

We both drank some chardonnay, and then he gestured for me to follow him outside—not to the patio with the outdoor living room where we'd sat and talked a few days earlier, but to a gorgeous dining area under a pergola, with grapevines providing shade and a view that looked down at the creek, all shimmering green cottonwoods and the slightly darker tones of oak and sycamore trees.

The table could seat eight, but only two place settings were laid out, with beautiful earth-toned stoneware that looked hand-glazed and heavy blown-glass goblets that had deep red rims, probably Mexican in origin.

"This is gorgeous," I said, eyeing the elegant tableware and the arrangement of autumn-hued roses and mums and greenery at the center of the table. "You did all this?"

A pleased light entered his eyes. Even though the sun was still bright, protected as we were under the pergola, he really didn't need to wear sunglasses. "Well, I ordered the flowers. But yeah, I set the table." Mouth quirking in amusement, he added, "What, you didn't think a pampered celebrity like me could set his own table?"

"That's not what I said," I told him in mock-severe tones, although the thought had entered my mind. Yes, when he was growing up here in Las Vegas, he'd been self-sufficient enough—heck, he'd managed to become an Eagle Scout on top of all his regular school activities—but ten years of being waited on hand and foot could change a person.

Not as much as I'd feared, apparently.

Little laugh lines appeared around his eyes as he grinned. "No, but you were thinking real loud."

About all I could do was stick my tongue out at him, and he chuckled. "I'll get the steaks going in a few minutes, but I thought we could sit down and relax a bit first."

That sounded like a good idea to me. Ever the gentleman, Max pulled out a chair for me and then took his own seat at the head of the table. For a minute or so, we sat there in silence, sipping chardonnay, feeling the warm breeze flow over us. Finches scolded each other in the trees that surrounded the house, and from far overhead came the sharp cry of a hawk. The finches went silent at once, but after it became clear that the hawk had business elsewhere, they started up their beeping chatter once again.

"So, what's the gossip around town?" he asked abruptly, breaking the silence.

I shrugged. "I don't know," I replied. "I mean, the coffee shop wasn't all that busy this afternoon, and I think people could tell I wasn't in any mood for chitchat."

"I don't blame you." Max drank some more of his chardonnay, then commented, "The world would be a much better place if people would just mind their own business."

Because I'd thought the same thing on more

than one occasion, I made a small sound of assent. Then I said, "But think of all those poor paparazzi who would be out of a job."

He actually laughed at that remark, as I'd sort of hoped he would.

"But it sounds as though the cast and crew are all heading home," I went on. "I guess the producers didn't have any interest in trying to find a different director."

"No, they wouldn't," Max replied. "Like I told you before, the project was really Perry's baby—he got the financing, co-wrote the script. A replacement director wouldn't be able to bring the same passion to the film. I'm sure they all thought it was better to cut and run, especially since he died so early in the production before much was shot."

I went quiet then, thinking of all the people who'd rearranged their lives to come here to Las Vegas to make the film, and who'd have to head home and figure out what to do next. At least they were getting paid, but....

A thought struck me, and I asked, "I heard something about a completion bond. That's like insurance for a movie, right?"

Max nodded. "Basically."

"Well, what if someone offed Perry for the insurance money?"

My friend's expression shifted, as though he'd been about to smile and then stopped himself, not wanting me to think he was mocking me. "It's not that kind of insurance," he said, but his tone was friendly, almost gentle. "It's just there to pay the investors their seed money back, and to fulfill the contracts of everyone who was working on the film. That's what most people in the film industry are—a bunch of contractors. We're hired for a specific project, and then we move on. Sure, the people who work directly for the studios have what you could call 'real' jobs with salaries and benefits and all that, but the rest of us are just a bunch of 1099 schmoes."

Schmoes who get paid eight figures, I thought, even though I knew most of the people who'd come here to work on *Perdition Row* earned a lot less than that. Max was in a rarefied class of people when it came to movie-star salaries.

Still, I couldn't quite let the thought go. "But what if there's someone who didn't want the movie made, for whatever reason? Getting rid of Perry would pretty much guarantee that the completion bond would have to be paid, right?"

Those questions made Max frown slightly...but then his expression eased, and he took another swallow of wine. "It's not impossible," he said. "But I think it's pretty improbable. The bond just guarantees the bare bones are covered. It's not going to make anyone money the way actually releasing the movie would."

I supposed that made sense. All the same, I had to wonder how big the box office would even be for a Prohibition-era drama, despite having one of the highest-paid actors in the world as its star. "You really think *Perdition Row* was going to make a lot of money?"

A flash of a grin, and Max said in wounded tones, "What, you don't think my name above the marquee is enough of a draw?"

Since I could tell he was teasing me, I gave an exaggerated shrug, even as I smiled. "I don't doubt you for a minute, Max. But it wasn't exactly your usual material."

"You're right. There's so much more to it than domestic box office, though—international receipts, sales to streaming services…it takes a lot of moving pieces to really figure out whether a film is profitable or not."

He was right, of course. Honestly, it all sounded pretty exhausting to me. I much preferred the straightforward nature of my own little business—it was easy to calculate what came in and what went out, whether I needed to make any adjustments or whether I could keep carrying on the same way I always had. Considering things really didn't fluctuate that much, it was pretty much "keep making coffee and carry on" when it came to making sure Levitation Latte stayed in the black.

No pun intended.

"Well, then, I'm fresh out of ideas," I said.

My complaint just made Max chuckle again. "So am I. But I suppose that's why I have Beverly on the case. I'll let her do the heavy lifting for now...and in the meantime, let's get those steaks going."

That sounded like a great idea to me. We both got up from the table and headed over to the outdoor kitchen, which was located only a few yards away from the pergola, and where a couple of steaks had been coming up to temperature, protected by plastic wrap as they waited on a plate.

Max got the steaks on the grill, along with some veggie kabobs, and once the food was well on its way, I went back into the kitchen to fetch the beans from the oven where they'd been keeping warm. When we sat down to eat, he talked about the ranch and about the weather, about projects he had coming down the pike—anything except his arraignment, or the trial that loomed in just a few weeks.

Trying to be normal.

I totally understood, and so I made sure to follow his lead, putting in comments here and there about the coffee shop, or about the harvest festival that would be coming up in the middle of October. Even that topic of conversation felt like something of a blunder, though, considering how his trial was supposed to start on October third, but he didn't call me out on it. No, he just said he might like to stick around for the event, since he wasn't scheduled to start filming his next movie until the second week of January.

"You should stay," I told him. "The festival's gotten much bigger since we graduated. We have a corn maze now and everything."

"Oh, a corn maze?" he replied with a grin. "I definitely can't miss that."

And so it went. After the meal ended—he definitely could grill a good steak—we took our plates into the kitchen and set them on the counter.

"Thanks for coming," Max said, his expression now quite serious.

"Dinner was great," I replied. "And you know I'll be here whenever you need me."

He made a brief movement, as if he'd been about to lay a hand on my arm and then had thought better of it. "Maybe that's why I was looking forward to coming back here," he said, and I lifted an eyebrow.

"What do you mean?"

"Because being in L.A., I almost forgot what it was like to have a real friend."

Heat touched my cheeks, and I desperately prayed he hadn't noticed my unwelcome reaction to his words. What in the world was I supposed to say to that?

Nothing of what was truly in my heart, that I loved being his friend but desperately wanted something more.

No, I just essayed a smile and replied, "I'll always be your friend, Max."

CHAPTER 12

The Stuff of Nightmares

Max walked me out to my car after that, and I waved goodbye before I headed down the winding lane to the gate, where another security guard—not Lou—motioned me through. I smiled at the man, although it was dark enough by then that I couldn't be sure he'd actually seen me.

Not that it probably mattered. The guy was there to work, and didn't need any distractions.

God knows I was distracted enough as I bumped my way along the dirt road that would lead me back to civilization. Maybe I shouldn't have had that last glass of wine, but I didn't think I was really too horribly tipsy, since I'd had a hearty dinner to go along with the cabernet Max had brought out to pair with the steaks.

No, it was more that I wished I could have

thought of exactly the right thing to say to him, the words that would let him know I wanted to be much more than friends while at the same time doing my best to make sure he didn't feel pressured by my revelations. In my mind, I could see him smile as he told me he'd been wanting the same thing and had been afraid to tell me because he didn't want to jeopardize our friendship.

Well, that was a nice fantasy. Too bad it would probably never come true.

I scowled as I jumped onto I-25 south to take the short hop that would bring me to the 7th Street off-ramp, and toward the heart of Las Vegas and the neighborhood where my house was located. As I merged onto the highway, though, I noticed a pair of headlights following me, staying just a little too close for comfort.

It's nothing, I told myself. *People heading back to town from the airport take this same route all the time.*

Nice explanation, but since the Las Vegas Municipal Airport was closed from dusk until dawn, no one should have been coming and going at this time of the evening, now almost nine o'clock.

My unease only increased as I turned off at 7th Street and the car behind me continued to follow a few yards behind my Subaru. Again, it could be nothing more than a coincidence, since my house was only a few blocks from Las Vegas's historic downtown, and yet....

All the businesses there would be closed except the Plaza Hotel. My hometown was definitely the kind of place where they rolled up the sidewalks after dark.

When I came to the spot where I should have made a right to turn into my neighborhood, I instead hung a left on National, aiming toward downtown...and the police station. No, Kyle wouldn't be working, since he'd clearly been assigned the day shift this week, but there would be someone to help me if necessary.

I pulled into the police station's parking lot and aimed for a space right in front of the building, next to an unoccupied handicapped spot. The car that had been following me paused at the entrance for a second or two, as if its driver was debating with himself whether to enter. Apparently, he decided that was a bad idea, because a moment later, my stalker sped up, moving toward Gonzalez Street, and I released a breath I hadn't even realized I'd been holding.

The police station's parking lot was brightly lit enough that I could see the vehicle was a late-model SUV, silver, with California plates. I couldn't tell who was driving, though.

California plates.

Someone with the cast or crew?

That didn't make a lot of sense.

Then I got it.

An over-ambitious paparazzo, someone who'd probably been waiting outside Max's rented ranch to see who was coming and going from the property. Max's security detail would have made sure that any interlopers couldn't get too close, but they certainly didn't have the power to prevent someone from parking on a public road.

Well, at least I'd shaken the guy off...for the time being.

Just to be safe, I waited in the police station parking lot for a good five minutes, then slowly edged out to the street, looking both ways in case the silver SUV with the California plates was lurking anywhere close. I didn't see it, though, and let out a little breath of relief as I pointed my car toward home.

Was I now going to have to look over my shoulder everywhere I went?

No one accosted me as I walked down the driveway to the back door of the house, and everything looked just as I'd left it, so it seemed the paparazzo hadn't figured out where I lived.

Yet.

I checked the locks on both the front and back

doors before I went upstairs to get ready for bed, and knew the house was as secure as I could make it. On mild late-summer nights like this one, I often left all the windows open, but I sure wasn't taking any chances like that on this particular evening. No, I'd make sure everything was shut and locked, and would just have to run the air conditioning to keep the place from getting too stuffy.

As I got ready for bed, I reflected there was something to be said for having the means to hire your own personal security escort. It would have been nice to know that Lou—or one of his counterparts—was standing guard at the front door, making sure no one got close.

But no, I really wouldn't want to live that way, having to watch everything I did, every place I went. All that money had given Max a nice prison, but it still felt like a prison nonetheless.

And if I didn't figure out what had really happened to Perry Lockhart...and soon...my friend might end up in an actual prison. As far as I could tell, the D.A. and Chief DeVargas both thought he was guilty, and so they weren't even bothering to look for another suspect.

It just seemed that everything I thought of, every angle I considered, ended up getting shot down in the end. Whoever had killed Perry Lockhart, they seemed to be a lot smarter than I was.

That might have been self-defeating talk, but I

had to admit I wasn't feeling very hopeful right then. What was really going on here? What detail had I missed?

If I hadn't been feeling so jangly, I might have gone downstairs and brewed some herbal tea, and put my best effort into attempting a reading. Somehow, though, I knew doing so would only be an exercise in futility. My brain wasn't in the right space at the moment to open itself to those kinds of vibes, and so the best thing to do was just go to bed, get some sleep, and hope I could start over in the morning.

I did pretty much pass out the second my head hit the pillow, since it had been a very long day. Unfortunately, my brain didn't seem to care that I really needed my rest.

The dream came swimming up out of the depths of my unconsciousness...or maybe it had come from much farther away. I still didn't know exactly where those true dreams originated. The only thing I did know was that I could always tell the difference between the ones that were more like visions and the ones that were simply a mash-up of incidents that had happened during the course of my day, or problems and worries that continued to plague me even after I went to sleep.

In my dream, I was walking through the aisles of the Lowe's Super Save, the only real market in town besides Walmart. My cart was filled with bags and bags of flour and sugar, not completely surprising, since I tended to go through those supplies fairly quickly.

Except I didn't buy the Levitation Latte supplies at the grocery store. Those staples were delivered every week by a bulk food supplier.

Well, it was a dream. It didn't have to make sense, even if it turned out to be one of my true ones.

Because the cart was full almost to the brim with such heavy items, it was very hard to push. One of the wheels wobbled, too, making my progress even slower. Just as I was about to approach the flour and spices aisle, Raylene Evans suddenly blocked my way.

She had an overloaded grocery cart in front of her as well, only hers was filled with boxes and boxes of Valentine's candy, all red bows and shiny metallic finishes.

My dream-self frowned, as if she knew it was early September and there was no way in the world Raylene should have been able to fill her cart with candy that wouldn't be available for another six months.

She stared down at all the flour in my own cart, and her mouth twisted. In my dream, she looked like the girl who'd tortured me in high school, and not the frazzled mom of three she'd become. Her blonde hair fell in perfect waves over her shoulders, and she wore her green and gold West Las Vegas High School cheerleading uniform.

Her mouth curled as she looked down at the piles of flour and sugar in my shopping cart. "None of that is going to do you any good, you know," she said.

My dream-self had been thinking roughly the same thing. Even though I somehow knew I was dreaming, I couldn't help being assailed by an overwhelming sense of futility.

Rather than address her comment directly, however, I only said, "Why do you have all that Valentine's candy?"

Raylene smiled—a smile as false and sticky-sweet as the candy in her cart. "Because everyone loves me. *He* loves me."

The little twist at the corner of her mouth told me exactly which "he" she was talking about. Never mind that she and Max hadn't been together for almost a decade, or that she was supposedly happily married with a family of her own. Of course, now I knew the truth, that she'd never really gotten over him and had apparently been willing to throw away everything she had in an attempt to reclaim what they'd once shared back in her high school glory days.

My dream-self smirked right back at her. "That's not what he told me."

At once, Raylene's expression grew stormy.

"You don't know what you're talking about," she snapped. "He loves me, and he'd do anything for me."

"Keep telling yourself that," I said, then began to push my shopping cart past her.

Enraged, she shoved me out of the way and grabbed hold of the handle, then turned the cart over, bags of flour and sugar flying everywhere, spilling their contents all over the store's linoleum floor. I stared down at the mess in dismay, wondering how I would ever be able to clean it all up, worried that the store manager would come over and make me pay for everything even though the current chaos in the aisle hadn't been my fault.

But even as I began to take a step toward Raylene, as though my dream-self intended to shake her or maybe even give her a smack on the arm as punishment for what she'd just done, I startled awake, my eyes flying open as I focused on the ceiling fan quietly twirling away over my head.

For a second or two, I just lay there, trying to get my bearings. The dream had felt horribly, horribly real.

Too real.

And that was how I knew it had been a vision of some kind, although I had absolutely no idea what it had been trying to tell me. I already knew about Raylene's continuing obsession with Max, so why should the dream have felt so important?

I didn't know.

Was Raylene the murderer?

No, that didn't make any sense at all.

Unless....

I sat up in bed, brain going a mile a minute, as though I hadn't been buried in the depths of REM sleep only a few minutes earlier.

What if Raylene was so angry at Max for blowing her off that she'd decided to frame him for murder as payback?

On the surface, that didn't seem like such a far-fetched idea. I knew my old nemesis could be absolutely unstoppable once she got the bit between her teeth.

But we were talking about a stay-at-home mother of three here. While she might have had plenty of motive, I wasn't sure she had the means... or the time. How in the world would she have ever been able to get her hands on that gun, let alone break into Perry Lockhart's Airbnb to do the deed? After all, the gun had been doubly locked up—first in the portable gun safe itself, and then in the storage unit where the safe was being kept. I had no doubt that a world-class thief would have been able to make short work of such a task, but this was Raylene Evans we were dealing with here, not the guy who stole the Pink Panther diamond back in the '60s, or whenever that particular heist had occurred.

Still....

Frowning, I got out of bed and grabbed a robe from the closet, wrapping it around myself as I made my way down the stairs. Since I was wide awake, I figured the best thing to do was make myself some chamomile tea, and hopefully it would put me back to sleep in short order. I might have been having prophetic dreams, and I might have had a pleasant evening at Max's ranch, but I still had to get up at a quarter to five and therefore needed to be back in bed as soon as possible.

Since I didn't want to waste any more time than I had to, I nuked hot water in a mug and got out a bag of Celestial Seasonings tea rather than doing everything from scratch. Soon enough, I had a cup of warm tea cradled between my hands as I headed out to the living room, figuring I'd sit down on the couch and drink the tea there, rather than sit at the kitchen table.

Some impulse made me go over to the front window and peer through the blinds before I sat down, though. And that was how I spotted that damn silver SUV, parked right out in front of my house.

A shock of cold went through me.

How the heck had he figured out where I lived?

He saw your license plate, my brain said in reasonable tones. *He probably looked it up somehow.*

Exactly how, I didn't know, although I

wouldn't put it past an ambitious paparazzo to get a private investigator's license so he'd have access to all kinds of informational databases. And I knew I kept thinking of the intruder as male, even though I supposed it was possible that the intrusive photographer might be a woman. For some reason, though, I didn't think a woman would be quite so invasive about my personal space.

And okay, some people would probably argue that being parked at the curb some ten yards or so from the house wasn't exactly invading my bubble. But that's what this felt like...an invasion, an intrusion.

Unfortunately, there didn't seem to be much I could do about it. I had no doubt if I called the police and told them about a strange car parked in front of my house, they'd probably inform me that I needed to call back when there was a real emergency.

Scowling, I stepped away from the window and went to the kitchen, which at least was at the back of the house, behind a fence and a gate. My hopes of the chamomile tea helping me to get a decent night's sleep were growing dimmer and dimmer, but I made myself sit down at the table there anyway and drink the whole cup. When I was done, I rinsed out the mug, put it in the dishwasher, and headed back upstairs, resolutely not looking toward the front window, quashing the impulse to peek outside and see if the silver SUV was still parked there.

Like the kitchen, the main bedroom was located to the rear of my home and overlooked the backyard. This also reassured me, since I wouldn't have to worry about the occupant of the SUV being able to glimpse my light getting turned off after I slipped into bed.

I lay there, eyes wide open as I stared at the ceiling. My nerves jangled and my thoughts raced, and I wondered if I'd ever be able to relax enough to fall asleep. The clock on my bedside table told me it was only ten-thirty, not so terribly late. Max was probably still awake. What if I called him and explained the situation, and asked if he could send one of his security team over to read the paparazzo the riot act?

No, that was a terrible idea. For one thing, I really didn't want him to know how rattled I was, and second, those security guards were there to keep watch over Max, who needed them way more than I did. While annoying, paparazzi knew their boundaries, which was why this particular one was staying in his SUV and hadn't tried creeping around in my backyard so he could try peering in my kitchen window while I sat there and drank my chamomile tea.

I had to believe eventually he'd get tired of waiting for me to do something interesting and would head back to whatever motel he was staying in while loitering around Las Vegas, trying to get some good photos he could sell to the *National Enquirer* or TMZ, or whatever other questionable outfit that earned its money by preying on the personal lives of people with the misfortune to be famous. In the meantime, I needed to get to sleep.

A few smacks of my pillow to get it into the shape I wanted, and I rolled over and closed my eyes.

To my immense surprise, I actually fell asleep.

My alarm went off at four forty-five the next morning, and I automatically reached over and smacked the button to turn it off, then blinked into the darkness. Resolved to go about my normal morning business, I climbed out of bed, took a shower and washed my hair, then headed downstairs about twenty minutes later to get myself some coffee and another leftover cornbread muffin.

It wasn't until I was fully dressed, teeth brushed and minimal makeup applied, that I allowed myself to walk into the living room and peek out past the blinds.

Damn it.

The silver SUV was still parked there. I couldn't see into the vehicle, naturally, because the sun wouldn't be up for another couple of hours, but I had to believe the paparazzo was inside. Had he slept there all night?

It sure looked that way. Not for the first time, I wished Las Vegas had overnight parking laws, or I could have at least contacted the police to let them know the vehicle was in violation of our local ordinances. As it was, my hands were tied.

And I really, really wished I'd taken the time to clear out the garage so I could park my Subaru inside. The garage was still full of my grandmother's stuff, belongings I just couldn't quite bring myself to sort through. Since the car was far from brand spanking new, I didn't really care if it sat out all night.

Or at least, I hadn't cared until I had a paparazzo parked in front of my house for the duration. If I'd been able to pull into the garage when I got home the night before, that would at least have created some uncertainty as to whether I was actually here or not. But he must have seen the Outback, and so was poised to pounce the second I backed out of the driveway.

Too bad I didn't own a pair of night-vision goggles. Then I could try to look inside the silver SUV and see if its occupant was still asleep, or whether he had woken up and was just sitting there and waiting for me to make my next move.

Well, I had a pair of binoculars. Better than nothing.

I went to the coat closet and got the binoculars down from their perch on the shelf. In the past, I'd mostly used them for bird-watching, but I had bigger prey in mind right now.

Moving carefully, I pushed up the bottom of the blinds, allowing myself to place the binoculars against the window so I could get a clear view of the SUV. The closest streetlight was halfway down the block, so I couldn't see anything too clearly. However, I thought I could make out the shape of someone in the front seat, their posture a little off kilter, as though they'd slumped over sideways when they'd fallen asleep sitting up.

Well, that was a small piece of good news. Maybe I'd be able to sneak out after all and have my stalker be none the wiser.

I returned the binoculars to the closet, then went back to the kitchen and scooped up my purse and keys, which I'd left sitting on the table when I'd come downstairs a few minutes earlier. Moving with extreme care, I let myself out the back door and locked it quietly behind me. The back steps always creaked a little, but I had to hope the noise wouldn't carry all the way out to the curb.

However, I kind of doubted I'd be able to conceal the sound of my Subaru's engine starting up, even though it was parked at the extreme end of the driveway, right in front of my overstuffed garage.

What to do?

I unlocked the car and set my purse on the passenger seat, frowning as I considered my conundrum. True, the paparazzo had looked pretty out of it—probably thanks to staying up until all hours, hoping I'd do something interesting—and so I supposed there was always the chance I could back out of the driveway as quickly as possible and then floor it as soon as I got to the street, but that plan sounded a little too risky. It was very early in the morning, so not too many people were out and about, and yet I knew Dave Margolis left home almost as early as I did, since he was on the early shift at the cement plant on the outskirts of town. And there was always the random chance of mowing down an innocent paperboy.

It looked like desperate times called for desperate measures.

The Subaru was old enough that it had an old-fashioned ignition, not the sort of thing you could start with the push of a button or a command from an electronic key fob, but in this particular case, that was a good thing.

I got in and released the parking brake and shifted the car into neutral, then hastily jumped back out so I could hold the steering wheel with one hand while I started rolling the Subaru down the driveway. Luckily, it had a very slight slope, so at least I wasn't trying to push the thing uphill.

And my stratagem actually seemed to be working. Once or twice, the car started to veer off into the grass to either side of the drive, but I managed to course-correct and keep it headed toward the street. Just before it was about to roll off the driveway and out into the road, I jumped behind the wheel, started the engine, and pointed the car toward downtown.

I'd halfway expected the silver SUV's lights to come on immediately, catching me before I'd completed my getaway, but it remained dark. Maybe the paparazzo was a very sound sleeper, or maybe he'd woken up barely in time to catch a glimpse of me before I disappeared around the corner. Either way, it seemed I'd managed to make my escape.

All the same, I didn't completely relax until I was safely inside the coffee shop, lights blazing even though we wouldn't be open for another hour and a half. I was tempted to turn on the alarm system until Deanne got there, but then thought better of it. The place was securely locked up, and I really didn't want to scare my friend out of her wits by having her trigger the alarm when she showed up in half an hour.

Instead, I got to work putting together the various batters for that day's offerings, and let the comforting ritual of gathering my ingredients and mixing them together help soothe my jangled nerves. By the time Deanne showed up, the muffins were in the oven, and I was treating myself to a chai latte.

"Hey," she said as she came in.

"Hey," I replied. While part of me wanted to skip right over the problem of the pesky paparazzo, I knew I needed to let my friend know what was going on, just in case he decided to branch out and start following anyone who had even the slightest connection to Max or me. "Did anyone follow you over here?"

"'Follow'?" Deanne repeated, her brows pulling together. As always, she wore light makeup, just enough to look put together without being over the top about it. "No, I don't think so. I mean, I didn't see anyone. It's still pretty dead out there at this hour. Why?"

I fortified myself with another sip of chai latte, and then explained how someone had followed me home from Max's place and then proceeded to camp out in front of my house all night. "I'm sure they're just trying to get whatever story they can," I added once I was done with my recitation. "But still, it's annoying...and creepy."

Deanne's frown had only deepened during all this. When I was done, she said, "You need to call the cops."

"About what?" I asked plaintively. "The guy's keeping his distance. It's not like he was sleeping on my porch or something."

"I don't care," she said as she went over to pour herself a cup of coffee. "It's still super creepy. I'm sure the police would do something if you let them know what was going on."

Maybe she was right. It probably wouldn't hurt to put the police on alert, just in case that paparazzo decided to step up his game and get a little more aggressive.

"I'll think about it," I said. "For now, though, we need to finish getting ready for opening."

So we got busy with putting together a batch of croissants in various flavors, along with some plain and some poppyseed bagels. By the time we were done, it was almost seven.

When I unlocked the doors, no one was lurking outside. Sure, I saw Mr. Turnbull coming down the street so he could pop in and get his usual venti Italian roast, but otherwise, Bridge Street looked pretty deserted.

So much for my fears that the paparazzo had figured out exactly where I'd gone, and had merely been waiting for me to unlock the doors so he could pounce.

I got Mr. Turnbull his coffee, and then the rest of our morning regulars started drifting in, everyone getting their drink of choice and its carb-heavy companion before heading out to start their day. After an hour had passed, I thought I could start to relax.

Bad idea.

A little after eight, a stranger walked in, and I knew immediately he was my stalker. Okay, the professional-looking camera with the long lens he had slung over one shoulder was a dead giveaway, although I assured myself that I would have recognized him even without it, since he had shifty dark eyes and pointy features that were just a little too rat-like for my taste.

As soon as he caught sight of me, he grabbed the camera and pointed it in my direction.

"Hey," Deanne said, neatly interposing herself between me and the interloper. "No cameras in here. Order something to drink, or leave."

Thank God that Deanne had two brothers, and so was a lot more physically fearless than I was. And obviously, the paparazzo was put off by her quick actions, because he stopped dead in the middle of the shop, a scowl creasing his sparse brows. "An espresso, then."

I hurried to work, while Deanne remained where she was, hands planted on her hips. Everything about her stance told me she was ready to do whatever was necessary to keep the guy from coming any closer to me, or deploying his camera again.

And obviously, he got the message, because he didn't try to move. No, he just stood there, squinty eyes looking even shiftier because of the way he kept frowning.

When I was done making his espresso, I handed it off to Deanne rather than getting any closer to the guy than I had to. "Three bucks," she said.

The guy dug in his pocket and got out some ones, then all but flung them at her. "You suck," he said distinctly, and stalked out the door.

"Have a nice day!" she called after him, her tone so sticky sweet, I probably could have used it to sweeten a mocha latte. After he let the door bang closed behind him, she turned back toward me.

"*Now* will you call the cops?"

CHAPTER 13

Severance Package

With some reluctance, I picked up the phone and called the non-emergency number at the Las Vegas police department. Suzanne Esquivel, another former classmate of ours, was the one answering the calls that morning, and she sounded suitably horrified after I related my tale of woe.

"The guy was sleeping out in front of your house all night?" she said. "And then he actually came into your shop?"

"Well, he didn't exactly *do* anything," I replied. Not that I was trying to defend the guy, but I also didn't want to blow the situation completely out of proportion.

"It's still totally creepy," Suzanne said, echoing Deanne's words of not an hour earlier.

Since I couldn't really argue with that observation, I just made a noncommittal sound.

"I'll send someone out to take your statement in a little bit," Suzanne went on. "But if the guy shows up again, call 9-1-1 and we'll have an officer out there ASAP."

I sort of hated the idea of wasting an emergency call on something that didn't feel like an emergency to me, but I told myself to take Suzanne's advice. After all, our little town wasn't exactly jumping with criminal activity, so they could probably spare an officer to come over and check things out.

"Okay," I said. "But I have a feeling he won't come back."

"Don't be too sure of that," she responded. "I've heard these guys can be pretty persistent. I mean, poor Max had to hire a security team just to keep them away while he's staying here."

Those words told me Suzanne was pretty thoroughly on Team Max—not that I had expected anything different. The judge might have found probable cause to go ahead with the arraignment, but that didn't mean most of Las Vegas's population agreed with him.

I made a sympathetic mumble, but I kept myself from mentioning that I knew all about Max's security guards because I'd been at his house the evening before. It was probably safe to assume the news about my visit had already made the rounds, and yet I didn't see the point in adding extra fuel to the fire.

"I'll definitely call if I see the guy again," I promised, and Suzanne told me to take care before ending the call.

After I put the handset back in the receiver, I turned to see Deanne watching me, her expression speculative. "So?"

"They told me to call if the guy shows up again," I said. "Other than that, there's not a whole lot else we can do."

Her expression was still troubled, but it seemed she was ready to let it go for now. After all, I'd done my due diligence. Now I just needed to get on with my day.

Which included having to deal with Raylene Bryant's husband Evan, who came in a little before ten and who wanted to take back a box full of muffins and a dozen coffees for the guys at the car dealership. Under different circumstances, I would have been fine with getting such a big order...but normally, Evan or his dad would have called in advance to let me know what they were planning so I could prepare myself and make sure I had enough stock on hand.

However, I did my best to hold back any sharp words on the subject of his short-sightedness. Whatever I might think of Evan—and to be perfectly frank, that wasn't a whole heck of a lot—I didn't want to antagonize a regular customer. Mine wasn't the only coffee shop in town, although I liked to believe it was definitely the best.

Deanne was irritated, too, I could tell, but she also did her best to be pleasant. "Big meeting today?" she asked as she started filling a box with the various muffins Evan had requested.

"No," he said, a smile that edged a little too much toward smirk-ville playing with his lips. Back in high school, I'd considered him moderately cute, with his thick brown hair and boyish features, but he'd gained quite a bit of weight over the past ten years, and his face had gotten somehow thick and slack as well. However, those alterations in his appearance didn't seem to have penetrated his consciousness, because he still acted like a guy who could have had his pick of our high school's cheerleaders. Actually, I was fairly sure he'd done pretty much that exact thing back in the day, considering some of the rumors I'd heard.

But rumors were rumors, and I generally tried my best to give people the benefit of the doubt. In Evan Bryant's case, though, that was a little harder than usual.

His gaze slid toward me where I stood by my trusty Breville, filling one go-cup after another with that morning's Sumatran blend. I couldn't tell exactly what was going on behind those hazel eyes, but I didn't think I liked it.

"We just decided to give the guys a treat," he went on in response to Deanne's question. "Sorry I didn't call first—we've been pretty slammed over there today."

Somehow I doubted the local Ford dealership was overflowing with customers on that particular Tuesday morning, but I didn't say anything. To me, this was clearly a case of Evan getting antsy and deciding he needed to get out and about, and so he was just using the excuse of coming to buy a midmorning treat for the staff as a way to take some time off.

"It's fine," I said, figuring I'd better speak up first before Deanne opened her mouth and started delivering a few home truths about how he should stop expecting people to drop everything and cater to his personal needs.

She shot me an exasperated look, but at least she didn't say anything, only put the last of the muffins inside the box and then sealed it shut with a piece of tape. Since I had just finished filling the last of the cups, I put them all in a couple of carry containers and then set them on the counter as well.

"That'll be eighty-two fifty," I said.

Evan handed over a corporate credit card, and I scanned it, then gave it back. The sale went through right away—not that I hadn't expected it to. I didn't know much about Evan and Raylene's finances, although he was always driving a brand-new truck or SUV—a perk of his job at his daddy's dealership, I assumed—but I knew that credit card was backed by the dealership itself and therefore good as gold.

When I turned around the tablet with its Square scanner that I used for credit card processing, Evan wore that same smirk as he traced his signature using the tip of his index finger. Once again, I thought I caught a flicker of something unpleasant in his eyes once he was done and he looked back up at me, but because the moment came and went so quickly, I tried to tell myself I was imagining things.

God knows I'd had enough happen to me that morning that I thought I'd earned my paranoia.

Deanne, bless her heart, helped Evan carry all the booty out to his car so I wouldn't have to deal with him any more than I already had. If asked, she probably would have said she just didn't want me risking another encounter with our annoying paparazzo, but she knew me well enough that she was also trying to save me from spending any more time in Evan Bryant's presence than I absolutely had to.

The guy just rubbed me the wrong way, and not only because he'd been Raylene's partner in tormenting me back in high school, probably because he'd been hoping to earn points with her and lure her away from Max.

His ploy hadn't worked at the time, but not for lack of trying. I often wondered if Raylene had married him because she'd run out of energy at fending him off.

Anyway, I allowed myself an inner sigh of relief once his big red F-150 pulled away from the curb outside the shop. Deanne came back inside, looked at the denuded bakery display case, and shook her head. "We should probably make more, right?"

Having to put together additional batches of pastries after the morning rush was always tricky, since the last thing I wanted was to have a bunch of leftover product on my hands. At the same time, I knew we couldn't go the rest of the day with only a few forlorn croissants and bagels in there.

"I'm on it," I said. "Hold down the fort out here, okay?"

She gave me a thumbs-up. "No problemo."

With the all-clear to head back into the kitchen and make some muffin magic, I went and gathered the ingredients for blueberry and apple spice muffins, since those were my two most popular flavors, and made a few dozen more. Hopefully, that would be enough to last us until three-thirty. If not, I'd just tell everyone that the guys at Bryant

Ford had wiped us out and that they needed to take up the matter with them.

And okay, I wouldn't *really* say such a thing to my customers...but it was tempting.

Luckily, late morning tended to be quiet, and so I was able to replenish our stock without inconveniencing anyone by making them wait because only one person was manning the front of the shop. After that, our foot traffic ebbed and flowed in pretty much the usual patterns, telling me the *Perdition Row* cast and crew must have checked out of the Plaza Hotel and returned from whence they came. I still didn't know whether having them all go back to California or wherever was such a great idea...I hadn't given up hope that one of them might be the real killer...but apparently, Chief DeVargas didn't hold my same view of the situation. No, with Max safely arraigned, she probably thought the matter was pretty much put to bed.

I didn't agree with her, obviously. But since the police chief hadn't called me to get my advice on the situation, I knew my thoughts on the matter didn't count for much.

At a little after one, I headed outside to wipe down the bistro tables, since the people who'd been occupying them had left behind a trail of crumbs and a couple of sticky-looking rings. Just as I was straightening up, task done, I spotted our annoying paparazzo.

He was parked across the street, camera with its huge telephoto lens pointed right at me. And although I couldn't hear it from this distance, I had no doubt he was clicking away, probably filled with glee that I wasn't exactly at my best right then, with my hair pulled back in a ponytail and the little bit of makeup I'd applied before leaving the house that morning now pretty much gone.

Okay, that did it.

I marched back inside and went over to the phone. Deanne had been in the middle of wiping off tables as well, and sent me a surprised look.

"What's the matter?"

"That guy," I said, pointing toward the coffee shop's front windows. "He was lying in wait, just sitting there and waiting to catch me when I came outside."

She glanced in the direction I'd indicated, and her eyes narrowed. "That guy needs to get a hobby."

"Seriously." I picked up the phone and dialed the police station again, ignoring Suzanne's advice to call 9-1-1. Even as ticked off as I was at the moment, I couldn't quite justify tying up the emergency line over something so trivial. The paparazzo hadn't made any threatening moves, but if nothing else, maybe the police could catch him on a parking violation. Because Bridge Street was something of a tourist attraction, you weren't supposed to park in any one spot for longer than two hours.

Once again, Suzanne answered. "Las Vegas Police Department, how can I help you?"

"Hi, Suzanne," I replied. "It's Skye again. Could you send someone over here? That paparazzi guy is loitering across the street and was taking pictures of me while I was outside, just trying to do my work."

"No problem," she said. "I'll get someone over there as soon as I can. Is the guy still in the same spot?"

I lifted the phone from my ear and leaned across the counter so I could peer out the coffee shop's open front door. The silver SUV remained in the place where I'd spotted it a few minutes earlier, although I couldn't see the driver from my vantage point.

"Yes, he's still there."

"Okay, we're on it. Hang tight."

"Thanks, Suzanne."

The call ended, I returned the handset to the receiver and turned back toward Deanne.

"Are they sending someone?"

I nodded. "Yep. Sounds like it shouldn't be too long."

"Good." She crossed her arms and stared out through the shop's front windows, her pink-glossed mouth tight with annoyance. "Maybe it's legal, but I hate that these guys can just follow people around and take photos of their lives without having to suffer any consequences. It's so intrusive."

No kidding. I knew a lot of time would have to pass before I stopped peeking out the windows of my house to make sure some random stranger wasn't parked there, trying to steal a slice of my life. And maybe it wasn't totally cool to be siccing the cops on this particular paparazzo, but I'd had enough. He needed to go camp somewhere else... preferably all the way back in Southern California. There had to be much better prey in Beverly Hills or whatever than he could find here in little old Las Vegas, New Mexico.

"I know," I said. "But help is on the way, so I guess we should just try to act normal in the meantime."

Deanne's expression was dubious, but she didn't argue. "Sure. I need to make another batch of iced tea, anyway."

Yes, the day was warm enough that we'd been going through it more quickly than usual. Whether we'd need a full batch when we would be closing in a little over two hours, I wasn't sure, but I didn't comment. At least the task would help to keep her busy.

A little less than ten minutes after I'd called the police department, I spied a black and white cruiser pulling up behind the silver SUV, which hadn't moved the entire time. Kyle Isaacs got out of the squad car and walked up to the driver-side window, then paused there. I could tell he was talking to the paparazzo, but from this distance, I couldn't hear what they were saying.

"Looks like the cavalry has arrived," Deanne remarked. She'd poured herself a glass of iced tea, and held it in one hand as she watched the exchange across the street with some interest.

Honestly, I'd never thought I'd be so glad to see Kyle Isaacs. Whatever he said to the paparazzo, it appeared to have the desired effect, because a moment later, the SUV's engine revved to life, and the guy pulled out and zoomed down Bridge Street at a rate of speed I wouldn't have thought advisable, considering a cop was watching the whole thing.

But it seemed Kyle was satisfied with the outcome, because after standing in place and watching the departing vehicle for a moment or two, he waited for a break in traffic and then crossed the street, a smile on his lips.

"Hey," he said as he entered the shop. "Dirtbag dispatched."

"Thank you so much," I replied, hoping he could recognize the heartfelt gratitude in my tone. "That guy was seriously giving me some bad vibes."

"Just doing my job," Kyle said, although he looked awfully cheerful for an on-duty cop.

"Still," I said, then paused. "Can I get you something? Coffee? A muffin?"

"One of those ham and cheese croissants would be great," he responded after a brief look at the contents of the bakery case. "We had to do a drug bust at the high school about an hour ago, so I didn't get much of a lunch."

"One croissant, coming up," I told him. Deanne had retreated to one of the tables near the window and was wiping it down with more gusto than the task probably required. She might have been trying to keep an eye out just in case the paparazzo returned, or she'd decided it was better to stay out of the way while Kyle and I had our convo. "Anything else? Tea?"

"Iced tea would be great," he said.

I poured him a cup and handed it across the counter. At once, he took a sip, and then helped himself to a bite of croissant. Although he'd been quick in coming out here, it didn't look as though he was in a big hurry to get back on patrol.

Well, considering the favor he'd just done for me, I was okay with that.

"Drug bust at the high school," I said. "Which one?"

"Robertson," Kyle said. That was Las Vegas's other high school, the one that was West Las Vegas

High's bitter rival, and a petty part of me was glad the arrests hadn't gone down at our alma mater. "It was small-time stuff, just weed. But it's still illegal for anyone under eighteen, so a couple of kids are probably going to end up in juvie over it."

Thank God it hadn't been meth or fentanyl or any of the other illegal substances that could make a real hash of people's lives. A little weed wasn't anything to get too bent over, even if it was only legal for adults in our state.

"Anyway," Kyle went on, "I'm glad I was able to swing by. I've got some news."

"'News'?" I repeated, not sure whether I really liked the sound of that.

He sipped some more of his iced tea, although it seemed he was ready to hold off taking another bite from the ham and cheese croissant he held until he'd delivered his momentous revelation. "You know how I told you that we'd gotten Perry Lockhart's laptop and phone, and were checking it for anything that might be relevant to the case?"

"Ye-es," I managed. An uneasy sensation began to swirl in the pit of my stomach, as if my body had somehow recognized this was going to be bad news even before I heard it.

"Well, our tech guy got into the laptop earlier today," Kyle said. "He found something that would have given Max Sullivan every reason to kill his director."

"What's that?" I asked, my tone guarded, even though I knew I needed to hear this unwelcome piece of information.

Kyle didn't exactly smile with glee, but I got the impression that he was enjoying this.

"Perry Lockhart was planning to fire him."

CHAPTER 14

Profit Motive

So much for my vow to myself that I wouldn't reveal anything to Max of what Kyle told me about the investigation. Nope, as soon as I locked the doors to Levitation Latte that afternoon and said goodbye to Deanne, I had my cell phone out and was sending a text.

We need to talk, I wrote. *Some new info just surfaced.*

At least Max didn't seem to be one of those people who left his phone in another room and didn't check it for hours. Almost as soon as I'd sent the message, he wrote back, *Come over now?*

Be there in 10.

He sent me a simple, "k," and I hurried into the back room to retrieve my purse and check on Tilly's food and water. Everything seemed to be ready for her next visit...whenever that turned out to be...and so I let myself out and got behind the wheel of my Subaru.

Before I exited the alley that backed up to the shop, I looked anxiously from side to side, worried that the silver SUV hadn't really disappeared from the scene but had only retreated to a less obvious location. However, I didn't spot the vehicle anywhere in the vicinity, and so I pulled into the street and headed east.

During the entire drive, I kept checking the rearview mirror and looking over my shoulder—an activity that almost made me rear-end a Toyota pickup when they stopped suddenly to allow someone to jaywalk across National Avenue—but I still didn't see the annoying paparazzo. Maybe Kyle really had put the fear of God in him.

Whatever the reason for my stalker's absence, I was able to make my way to the turn-off for Max's rented ranch without anyone tailing me or appearing to take any particular interest in where I was going. When I pulled up to the gate, it was to find Lou standing there.

His expression was a little less intimidating than it had been during my first visit, possibly because I was now a known quantity. "You can go right up," he said. "Mr. Sullivan is waiting for you."

Pretty much the same exchange as the first time I'd come here, and yet I still found it reassuring that I hadn't been challenged in any way. I said, "thanks so much," and then continued along the narrow lane that wound its way through the property. As before, I found myself wondering just how big this place was. A couple hundred acres at least, making it exactly the kind of secluded spot a Hollywood celebrity in hiding might want.

This time, though, Max was standing outside the house. Apparently, Lou hadn't been joking when he'd said his boss was waiting for me.

I parked in front of the garage and got out of my Subaru. Although I'd been in a hurry to leave the coffee shop and come see Max, that haste hadn't prevented me from brushing my hair, blotting my nose with a sheet of rice paper from the little packet I kept in my purse, and applying a fresh coat of lip gloss. Whether any of that primping would have any effect on him was debatable, but at least I felt a little more confident as I approached him where he stood under the portico that sheltered the front door.

Being Max, he didn't seem too concerned that I was in possession of information important enough to come running over here the second I got off work. "How was the drive?" he asked.

"It was fine," I said. "At least this time, I didn't have any paparazzi following me."

His brow furrowed just the tiniest bit. "Excuse me?"

"Long story."

At once, his expression cleared. "Well, I've got some sangria waiting for us. Let's pour a couple of glasses, and then you can tell me all about it out on the patio."

Of course he had sangria. Then again, what else did he have to do with his time while he sat here and waited for the trial to roll around?

I told myself he probably had plenty of things to keep him occupied—consults with his attorney, probably some damage-control sessions with his agent and manager and PR person, and whoever else he kept on staff to maintain his squeaky-clean public image.

Not that it was so squeaky at the moment.

A brief detour into the kitchen to pour some glasses of sangria from a gorgeous pitcher that matched our blown-glass goblets from Mexico, and then we headed out to the patio. Just like the last time we'd sat out here, the weather was picture-perfect—the sky blue with just a few clouds floating past, the breeze warm and inviting. It was hard to believe October was now only a few weeks away, although our mild weather often lasted midway into that month.

After we'd both sat down in the outdoor living room, Max on the sofa and me on the love seat, he said, "So, what's this about the paparazzi?"

Just as I had with Deanne earlier that day, I explained about the guy who'd been camped out in front of my house, and how I'd done my best to ditch him but obviously hadn't been successful, considering the way he'd shown up at the coffee shop only a few hours later.

"It wasn't that he did anything exactly threatening," I concluded. "But just having him around was creeping both Deanne and me out. So, I called the cops on him."

"Good," Max observed, and then swallowed some sangria. "I'm sorry about that."

"'Sorry'?" I repeated as I gave him a blank look. "Why should you be sorry?"

"Because if it weren't for me, that guy would never have been following you around in the first place." He paused there, his expression irritated. "One of the things they do is try to prey on the people around a celebrity, follow them around in case they can dig up something interesting. I probably should have warned you."

"It's okay," I said. "It's not as though you haven't had a lot on your mind."

"Still."

If we'd had a different kind of relationship, I might have reached over and given him a reassuring pat on the knee or something. As it was, I had to settle for shrugging before I sipped some of my own sangria. It was excellent, full of fresh fruit flavors, but with a definite kick that told me he'd poured some brandy in there in addition to the red wine.

I'd have to make sure I only had this one glass. It definitely wouldn't do for me to be even a little off balance as I left the property, just in case any more intrepid photographers were lying in wait, trying to see if they could get their own photos of the mysterious woman who kept coming and going from Max Sullivan's rented ranch with such regularity.

Too bad for them that the reality was a whole lot less salacious than what they were probably thinking.

There wasn't any easy way to ask, and so I just blurted, "Did you know that Perry Lockhart was thinking of firing you?"

Max stared at me as if I'd lost my mind. "What?"

I supposed I could forgive him for looking so shocked. Speaking quickly, I replied, "My contact on the police force told me their investigators found evidence on Perry Lockhart's laptop indicating he wanted you off the movie."

Still looking as though someone had smacked him upside the head with a wet fish, Max waggled his jaw for a second, and then said, "Your 'contact'? What is this, the CIA?"

Despite the circumstances, I had to smile a little. "I'm not going to tell you their name because

I don't want them to get in any trouble for telling me this stuff. And I don't have a lot of details, so I can't tell you what exactly was found. But my contact seemed to think the evidence was pretty incriminating."

"It would provide a motive...I guess," Max responded. He drank some sangria, a bigger swallow than the last one. "On the other hand, losing a role generally isn't the sort of thing that leads to homicide."

"Have you ever been let go from a movie job?" I asked then. I didn't think so, but I also hadn't memorized every single detail of his career. It was entirely possible he'd been hired during the pre-production stage of a film and then had been quietly dismissed when the director realized he wouldn't be a good fit.

"Never," he said without hesitation. "And I don't know why Perry wouldn't have talked to me if he wasn't feeling the vibe. We're all grown-ups, you know."

Well, Max mostly acted like a grown-up. From what I'd seen of Perry Lockhart, I thought he'd had the petulant child thing pretty well down pat.

"It would also explain why he was being so brutal to you on set, though," I ventured. "Maybe he wanted to let you go but the producers wouldn't go along with the plan."

A few seconds passed as Max absorbed this

theory, and then he inclined his head ever so slightly, reluctance clear in the shadow that went over his face. "I suppose I can see that," he said. "I mean, it was the studios who prevailed on Perry to hire me in the first place. It was pretty obvious they were worried the film would be a flop if they didn't have some box-office muscle in the person they cast as the lead."

"And so Perry did whatever he could to make your life hell during filming," I went on. "He must have been trying to work up a case for getting rid of you by making it seem as though you couldn't get anything right."

"Jackass," Max muttered, and sipped some more sangria.

I couldn't really argue with that description of his former director. If Perry really hadn't wanted Max in the lead role, he should have just put his foot down.

But then, it was easy for me to make that kind of judgment about the situation, since I'd never had to operate under that kind of pressure. I wouldn't pretend to know anything about the machinations behind producing a big-ticket Hollywood movie, but I had to believe it could get pretty cutthroat when millions and millions of dollars were involved.

Because I'd delivered my bad news and now didn't really know what I should do next, I also drank some sangria. We sat in uncomfortable silence for a few moments, and then Max set down his glass and actually smiled.

"Thanks for telling me about this," he said. "I know it doesn't look good on the surface, but I'm sure Beverly will know how to handle it."

"I suppose that's why you pay her the big bucks," I replied, trying to keep my tone light.

"Exactly. And the thing is, they might have found evidence on Perry's computer that he was planning to can me, but unless they can produce a letter or an email or a recording of a voicemail or conversation that proves he actually talked to me about it, I don't see how this evidence is going to help them in the long run."

Being so optimistic definitely was an impressive skill. But then, Max's life had always gone the way he wanted it to. Not because he was the sort of person to browbeat or bully people, or to cheat or gaslight or do any of a hundred other kinds of underhanded stuff that was often employed by unscrupulous people, but simply because he just seemed to be blessed, like all the fairies had been able to deliver their gifts of luck and beauty and charisma without getting interrupted by the one bad fairy who would put the kibosh on the whole thing. Quite literally, this was probably the first time in his life when he'd had to confront a situation he couldn't charm away.

I realized then that Max needed to believe everything was going to be okay, that this was all just a misunderstanding that could be cleared up by a careful application of common sense and belief in the goodness of people. Very likely, he would find it difficult—if not impossible—to believe there were those who would look at the evidence and think he had to be guilty, just because they very well might have been driven to murder under similar circumstances.

Well, I told myself, *just make sure this never goes to trial, and then you won't have to worry about a bunch of jurors taking this so-called "evidence" the wrong way.*

Sure. I'd get right on that.

"True, this piece of evidence might not help," I said diplomatically. "I suppose that's for your attorney to figure out. But I wanted to make sure you had as much information in hand as possible so you wouldn't get blindsided."

"And I appreciate that," Max replied, now leaning forward a little bit, as though he wanted to make sure I recognized his sincerity. "Honestly, this would have all been a hell of a lot harder to deal with if I didn't know you were in my corner."

"I am," I said, praying I wouldn't blush at his words. Not for the first time, I wished I'd inherited my mother's olive complexion rather than the fair skin from my father's side of the family, which seemed to show everything. "And so are a lot of other people. We're all rooting for you." I stopped there, and sent him a quick glance from beneath my eyelashes. "How're your parents holding up?"

He didn't quite grimace, but I could tell he wasn't entirely happy I'd asked the question. "About as well as you might think. I mean, they know I didn't do it, but they keep having to field questions, and my mom's having the hardest time of it."

I could imagine. Tina Sullivan was the assistant principal at West Las Vegas Middle School, and I could only imagine the crap she probably had to deal with on a daily basis. Thirteen-year-olds weren't exactly known for their tact at the best of times, and for one of their school's authority figures to have a son accused of murder?

No, thanks. I'd rather be chased by paparazzi until the end of my days.

Ian Sullivan owned a contracting company, so that meant he was his own boss and could shut down any lines of questioning that got too out of hand. At the same time, he might have lost a few contracts over this whole mess. I wouldn't ask, though; that sort of thing was between Max and his parents. If any kind of work shortfall caused a problem for them, I had to imagine he would step in and help out.

At least being accused of murder hadn't put a dent in his enormous bank accounts...yet.

"I'm sorry," I said quietly. A wholly inadequate comment, but I had to hope he understood. "We're going to get this all straightened out, and then everything will go back to normal."

"'Normal,'" Max repeated in musing tones. "That would be nice."

Since I wasn't sure of the best way to respond, I instead lifted my glass of sangria. Just as I was about to take a sip, Max's phone—which had been sitting on the stone coffee table in front of us—rang. He grimaced and looked down at the phone's screen.

"My agent," he said. "I need to take this."

"No problem," I told him, and then allowed myself a delayed swallow of sangria.

As I settled against the back of the love seat where I was sitting, Max picked up the phone and held it to his ear. "Hi, Margaret. I—"

He stopped there, making me think his agent had cut him off before he could go any further. Then his face went curiously blank, the half-smile he'd been wearing disappearing as though someone had just swiped an eraser over his face.

Since I wasn't sure what else to do, I sipped some more sangria and then made myself gaze out at the dry hillsides around us, the shimmering green leaves of the cottonwood trees lining the creek that cut through the property. I had no idea what Max's agent was calling about, but I had to believe it wasn't anything good.

At length he said, "Sure, sure. I understand. No, I'll be here until after the trial. Thanks."

And he took the phone away from his ear and set it down on the table before picking up his own glass of sangria and taking a very large swallow.

Uh-oh. Not that I needed to worry about Max drinking—it wasn't as though he needed to drive anywhere after this—but he was usually more careful than that.

I waited in uneasy silence, knowing I needed to let him speak first.

Another swallow of sangria, and then he took a breath and said, "They just dropped me from my next film."

Oh, no. I stared at him and replied, "They can do that?"

He sent me a grim smile, but at least he set down his glass rather than fortifying himself with yet another gulp of his high-octane drink. "Sure. We hadn't started filming yet, and there's always some kind of escape clause written into a contract. The studio execs just thought it was a good idea to get someone else in the role, considering how up in the air everything is."

His voice was way too calm. I could tell he was doing everything he could to hold it together rather than vent his anger and frustration in front of me.

I began, "I thought you said filming doesn't start until January—"

Still in that preternaturally calm tone, he broke in, "It doesn't. But they're already in pre-production, and they just don't want the movie associated with someone who's accused of murder."

"We're going to clear your name," I protested, and he only gave a weary lift of his shoulders.

"Maybe," he said. "But the studio needed to make a decision now, and so I'm out." He released a breath, and his mouth tightened. "Seriously, I'm starting to think I'm cursed."

"Sounds more like bad luck to me," I commented, and he raised an eyebrow, looking a little more like himself.

"You don't believe in curses?" he asked. His tone was serious enough that I could tell he expected an equally serious response. "Even though you can read the future in tea leaves?"

"It's not exactly reading the future," I responded. "Like I said, it's more like getting hints. Anyway, that's a far cry from making a voodoo doll and sticking pins in it, or whatever."

Now he actually smiled. "I suppose that makes sense. Still, I think I'd rather believe someone back in Hollywood decided to take the wind of out my sails by casting a curse on me than think my luck has suddenly taken a sharp turn into the crapper."

Considering he'd been surrounded by a halo of good luck pretty much his entire life, I could see why he might think that. And while I honestly didn't know whether curses or hexes or whatever you wanted to call them were a real thing, what I did know was that my best and oldest friend definitely hadn't been able to catch a break lately.

I needed to change that...as soon as humanly possible.

Before I could respond, Max's phone rang again. His mouth twisted, and I could tell he didn't want to look down at the screen.

Habit won out, though, and he glanced at his phone. "Oh, hell. It's my lawyer. I really need to take this."

"It's fine," I said. No way in the world would I tell him to blow off a call from his attorney.

He picked up the phone and said, "Hi, Beverly." A pause while he listened, and then he replied, "No, that's okay. I actually have some new information I need to talk to you about. Just a sec." He put his hand over the microphone and looked at me, his expression apologetic. "Sorry, Skye. Beverly wants to come over and talk strategy, so—"

"It's fine," I said at once, and set down my glass of sangria. "You can tell her about what they found on Perry's laptop."

A grin. "That's the plan."

His moment of melancholy appeared to have departed as quickly as it had come, and that made me feel a little better. This was the Max I knew and loved, the guy who always needed to be acting, needed to be moving forward.

"I'll let myself out," I said, and he gave me a grateful nod as he moved his hand from the phone and spoke again.

"Sure, Beverly. Come on over."

I slung my purse over my shoulder and waved, then made my way through the house and out to the spot where I'd parked my car. The whole way, I fought my disappointment, telling myself I'd delivered the information about Perry's laptop to Max and that it was clear he now had more important claims on his time.

And I couldn't help feeling a bit guilty for sharing that information at all, even though I'd done my best to conceal exactly who my informant was. If Kyle had known I was going to run off to Max at the first opportunity and spill the beans, he probably wouldn't have said anything at all.

But I tried to console myself that all this would come out in discovery anyway, so the most I'd done was give Max a jump on things. For all I knew, his lawyer was calling because she'd just gotten those same facts from the Las Vegas P.D.

Lou was still standing guard as I left—no big

surprise, since I'd only been at the ranch for about forty-five minutes at the most—and I waved to him as I drove past. No hint of surprise on his broad features at my early departure, but I supposed someone who worked security for the rich and famous was probably used to keeping his thoughts to himself.

No sign of the paparazzo, either. My drive back to the house was uneventful, and I pulled into the driveway and went into the house via the back porch without having to worry about getting tackled.

In fact, the whole episode felt oddly anticlimactic. I wasn't sure what I'd been expecting, but whatever it was, it sure hadn't happened.

Usually when I got home from work, I'd put my feet up for a while and let myself relax into watching something mindless on TV. Right then, however, I knew I was in no mood for such a time-wasting activity. I hated the thought of Max losing work over this awful misunderstanding.

I needed to do something.

And all right, I guessed that a lot of people would argue he wasn't exactly in danger of ending up on the street, considering he'd earned close to a hundred million dollars over the past eight or nine years, but still. If one studio bailed out, then I had to believe others would follow soon enough.

The bleeding needed to be stanched ASAP.

Easy for me to say. I wasn't his lawyer, or a cop, or anyone who could be remotely useful in this kind of situation.

No, but I was someone with an odd little gift... and now was the time to use it.

Mouth set, I headed into the kitchen.

Time for tea.

CHAPTER 15

Hungry Like the Wolf

I went for an herbal tea this time, partly because the gunpowder green tea hadn't seemed to help me out very much, and partly because I was feeling a little tired after that glass of sangria I'd drunk. In most cases, caffeine in the form of some oolong tea might have seemed like the logical response to my wine ennui, and yet I didn't want to be seesawing back and forth between depressants and stimulants. A nice, fruity herb tea with some thick, chunky leaves seemed to be the better choice.

After rooting around in the pantry a bit, I decided on the raspberry hibiscus, partly because it had a nice, tart taste and a gorgeous color, and partly because the hibiscus petals tended to drape nicely against the side of my teacup. As I brewed the tea and then sat down at the kitchen table, I pleaded with the universe to send me a sign, anything that would lead me to Perry Lockhart's real killer and prove Max's innocence.

At the same time, though, I tried not to feel too desperate. Stress always interfered with a reading, and I knew if I allowed my personal feelings to intrude too much, I might end up with a blob that was even less helpful than the heart I'd seen in my last attempt at interpreting the leaves.

The tea smelled wonderful, full of fruit without being sticky-sweet. Once again, I followed the ritual of turning the cup around three times, and then made myself sit there and sip it slowly, watching as my backyard slowly warmed with the colors of approaching sunset.

When the tea was nearly gone, I set the saucer on top of the cup and inverted it, allowing the last few drops to drip onto the dish. I focused as deeply as I could before I pulled the saucer away, revealing the leaves stuck to the inner surface of the cup.

They definitely formed more distinct patterns this time, that was for sure. One was an almost perfect oval, and I frowned at it. Most of the time, an oval signified fertility, since it echoed the shape of an egg. However, since I didn't have a family and wasn't thinking of starting one any time soon—not with my dating life in the dumps and Max roiling up feelings I'd spend years trying to suppress—I couldn't think of why such a shape would have revealed itself now.

Unless Deanne was pregnant. She'd sworn up and down that she had no intention of having a baby until she was at least thirty, but sometimes biology didn't always behave the way we wanted it to.

But even if my best friend did turn out to be pregnant, I failed to see how that particular fact could have any connection to Perry Lockhart's murder.

Unless...he'd gotten someone pregnant, and she'd shot him when he told her he wouldn't have anything to do with her or the baby.

While that scenario sounded to me like something the erstwhile Mr. Lockhart might do, it still circled back to the fundamental problem of access to the weapon. I didn't see how an angry ex-lover could have gotten her hands on Max's on-screen gun.

And while I didn't pretend to be psychic— well, not *psychic*, psychic, like the kind of person who could walk into a house and immediately tell it was haunted, or who could read people's thoughts or whatever—I did have fairly good instincts regarding my readings, and something was telling me the pregnant ex-lover theory veered onto entirely the wrong track. I didn't pretend to understand everything that was going on here, but that wasn't it.

Okay, then.

Leaving aside the problematic oval, I gazed down into the cup again, eyes tracing the outlines of the leaves there. Quite a few of them made blobs without any real significance, but there was one about halfway up the cup, a small mass with little bits of leaf that looked like ears, and another piece that resembled a snout more than anything else.

In fact, it looked remarkably like a wolf.

A wolf was pretty much always a positive omen in tasseography. Its current position on the inside surface of the cup seemed to indicate I was going to be playing the good friend, helping other people with their troubles.

Well, that was pretty much exactly what I'd been doing for Max, and yet I couldn't shake the feeling I should be getting a different meaning from the wolf head that had revealed itself within the leaves.

But what?

Frowning, I got up from the table so I could fetch myself a glass of ice water. Technically, you weren't supposed to walk away in the middle of a reading like this, but the fruity tea had made me thirsty for plain water. Besides, I'd already performed the key parts of the ritual.

Now I just had to figure out what they meant.

After a few swallows of water, I stared back down into the cup. Yes, that was definitely a stylized wolf's head, snout long, ears flattened. In fact, it seemed to remind me of something I'd seen before, although I couldn't say what.

Why was the wolf important?

Unfortunately, it seemed as though the longer I wracked my brain, the less I was able to come up with. It was like those times back in trig where the formulas had seemed to dance right behind my eyes but couldn't make their way down through my fingers and into my pencil.

Good thing I really didn't need a good grasp of trigonometry to run a coffee shop.

Since sitting there and staring down into the cup clearly wasn't going to help me much, I got up again, only this time I took my glass of water into the living room. Television hadn't seemed too appealing a half hour earlier, but now I knew I needed to give my brain a rest. Either my sluggish synapses would finally make the connection, or they wouldn't. Trying to brute-force the issue was only going to frustrate me and make the solution that much more difficult to find.

I sat down and started flipping through the channels. My grandmother had DirecTV hooked up a couple of years before she passed, and even though I kept telling myself I needed to cancel the service and just rely on streaming the channels I wanted through a Roku device or something, I'd never gotten around to actually doing the deed.

That was why I had a bunch of stations I hardly ever watched, including the "local" news out of Albuquerque. Since the state's biggest city was a hundred miles away, most of what went on there didn't have much significance for me.

I was just about to move past the local ABC affiliate's five o'clock news when the announcer said, "And here's today's Lobos update."

My entire body went rigid with shock, and I stared at the TV screen, watching as the logo of a wolf's head with flattened ears and bared teeth appeared for a second or two before they moved on to a discussion of the previous night's pre-season football game.

The University of New Mexico's mascot was a wolf.

Since I'd never gone to school there, I supposed I could have been forgiven for not making the connection immediately. All the same, it seemed like way too important a clue to overlook.

Or maybe it wasn't that important at all. Max had gone to UNM, and maybe that was what the leaves had been trying to tell me and nothing more.

Once again, though, that particular thought

didn't feel right. The connection seemed much more immediate than that.

"All right," I said aloud. "Who else from Max's class went to school in Albuquerque?"

If I was even correct in limiting my search to members of his graduating class and no one else. Maybe the murderer had gone to UNM some twenty years earlier.

No, I didn't believe that. There was some reason why the leaves had shown me the wolf, a thread I just wasn't picking up yet.

Luckily, all my high school yearbooks resided on the bottom shelf of the antique bookcase in the living room. I hoped that by pulling out the one from my junior year and taking a look at the senior class, something might jog my memory.

Yearbook in hand, I returned to the couch, then flipped back to the pages that contained the photos of Max's class. Compared to a lot of places, our high school was pretty small, with only about a hundred or so students in each year. Going through them wouldn't take too much time.

Up near the front was Raylene, since her maiden name had been Brown. In fact, her picture was right next to Evan's, since his last name was Bryant. Maybe the placement had been a sign to him that they were meant to be together, although it sounded as though she'd needed a bit more convincing than a mere accident of alphabetization.

Wait a second....

Evan had also gone to UNM, barely squeaking in with an assist from his extracurricular activities, since the guy wasn't exactly what you could call National Merit Scholar material. He'd played football at the university, while Max had decided to focus on acting and leave his quarterback days behind him.

But while neither of them had graduated, Max had made it through to the end of his sophomore year before being discovered and heading off to Los Angeles. Evan, on the other hand, had barely squeaked through to continue as a sophomore, and then had dropped out only a few months in. His father had suffered a minor heart attack around the same time, and the story the family put out was that Evan had left college so he could help out at the dealership, but I'd had my doubts. Most likely, he'd been failing and had used his father's health as an excuse to leave school so he wouldn't have to admit to anyone that his grades had sunk him.

Was Evan the Lobo—the wolf—the tea leaves were warning me about?

Maybe. I'd never liked the guy, so I didn't have a problem believing the worst about him.

Jumping to conclusions, Skye, I scolded myself. *Keep going—you're barely through the alphabet.*

Resolutely, I kept flipping pages, doing my best to dredge up from the memory banks any recollections I might have had about who'd gone away to college. Las Vegas was a pretty blue-collar town, so it wasn't as though we boasted a lot of Ivy League candidates among our ranks. There was Cheryl Cathcart, who'd gotten a scholarship to Stanford, and there was Lewis Mondragon, who was an amazing violinist and who had gotten a full ride at Juilliard.

And there was Shawn Zales, who'd also gone to UNM on a football scholarship. He'd been our team's wide receiver, and a huge friend of Evan's. In fact, if a couple of our football players had gotten caught doing something squirrelly together, it was usually Shawn and Evan.

Like Evan, Matt hadn't made it too far at UNM. In his case, though, it was because an awful rotator cuff injury had pretty much benched him his freshman year, and he'd returned to Las Vegas after realizing his days of football glory had ended before they'd even really begun. I'd sort of lost track of the guy over the years, since we'd never really been friends, although every once in a great while I'd see him at Walmart or something.

Of course, trying to view him as a suspect didn't make much sense. He and Max hadn't been besties, but they'd always gotten along, and I certainly couldn't figure out why he would have had anything to do with Perry Lockhart.

Still, maybe there was a connection I just hadn't made yet. At least I knew for a fact that Shawn had gone to UNM and played on the football team, and so that definitely made him a Lobo. Now I just had to figure out why he might be important.

And pray that discovering such an all-important fact wouldn't take me too long.

I tried searching for Shawn Zales online but didn't find much—a couple of old articles about his time on the Lobos football team, and that was about it. Nothing on Facebook or Instagram, so whatever he was up to these days, it obviously was something that kept him off social media.

Or maybe he was one of those people who didn't see the need to post fifty different pictures of his breakfast, or whatever. I had an Instagram account for the coffee shop, but because I was so busy most of the time, I kept forgetting to do anything with it. It didn't seem too improbable that Shawn might be similarly blasé about the whole thing.

And I almost picked up my phone to send Deanne a text to ask her about Shawn, but then I remembered she and Mike were going over to his parents' house for dinner that night. Because I didn't want to interrupt her with something that might turn out to be not so important after all, I told myself I could ask her the next morning.

Under most circumstances, my plan should have worked out just fine. I knew I was feeling urgent, but I also had to tell myself that Max's trial wouldn't be happening for almost three weeks, so a delay of a single night wouldn't exactly be the end of the world. Unfortunately, she sent me a text early the next morning telling me she'd cracked a crown at dinner the night before and had to make an emergency trip to the dentist.

Be in as soon as I can, she added. *Sorry!*

I told her not to worry about it, even though I was inwardly chafing at yet another delay. But at least she hadn't said she needed to take the entire day off, and once again I scolded myself for being so impatient.

Maybe I could have asked Max about Shawn, but I didn't want to raise his suspicions if this turned out to be yet another dead end. Better to poke at it on my own and see if I could come up with something useful rather than get his hopes up over nothing.

In the meantime, I tried doing a few more internet searches on my phone in between customers, but again, all that effort yielded a big fat zero. And because I had to man the coffee shop myself until Deanne arrived, it meant I honestly didn't have a lot of free time to dig up dirt on Shawn Zales...if such dirt even existed at all.

Deanne finally showed up a bit past one, looking apologetic and a little puffy. "I am so, so sorry," she said breathlessly as she hurried in. "Dr. Owens was supposed to take me at eleven, but then he kept having emergency after emergency—"

"It's okay," I assured her. No point in beating herself up over something that wasn't even her fault. And because it was a Friday, things had been pretty busy, but again, she couldn't control the coffee shop's foot traffic. "I was able to hold down the fort. How's the tooth?"

She grimaced. "It's okay. He put on a tempo-rary crown to hold me for now, but I need to go back in a week. I made the appointment for a Wednesday, though, since that's usually our slowest day."

Once again, I told her it was fine and she could take as much time off as she needed. I waited until after she'd gone in the back to grab an apron and had returned to the counter before I ventured, "Hey, do you remember Shawn Zales?"

"Sure," she said. "Wide receiver, went to UNM, right?"

Just another thing I loved about my friend—she was amazing with names and faces, could remember all sorts of details about pretty much everyone she'd ever encountered, even if those meetings had been brief. That was why I'd really been hoping to pick her brain...I knew her recall would be much more detailed than mine.

"Do you know what happened to him after he had to drop out of college and come back to Las Vegas?"

Deanne frowned, mouth pursing slightly as she dipped into the memory banks. "Um...I know he's kind of bounced around at a bunch of different jobs." Her expression brightened, and she added, "Oh, you know that new storage facility they built up on Cinder Road? I heard he's the manager."

With those words, everything clicked into place with a certainty I could feel in the depths of my gut. No, I didn't know for sure that the storage place Deanne had just mentioned was the one where the *Perdition Row* prop master had decided to store the production's guns and other props, but the theory made sense—it would have been a little closer to where the bulk of the shooting was being done than Las Vegas's two other storage facilities, and therefore a lot more convenient.

My expression must have shifted, because she asked, "What is it? Why did you want to know about where Shawn Zales is working?"

Because I didn't know for sure whether my suspicions would turn out to be true, I thought it better to keep them to myself for the time being. "Oh, just something I was thinking about, and I figured you might know." Trying not to be too obvious, I shot a sideways glance at the clock that hung on the wall opposite the bakery counter. Only one-thirty, which meant I had two hours before I could close the coffee shop and hurry off to the storage place to find out whether my suspicions were true. And since Deanne could already tell something was up, I knew if I said I had to leave early to handle something, she'd put two and two together right away...and most likely want to tag along on my errand. While having her as backup had its appeal, I knew I needed to do this alone. If the two of us appeared at the storage facility together, Shane would probably realize we had an ulterior motive for our visit and most likely clam up.

Well, waiting another couple of hours wouldn't be the end of the world. I guessed that the storage facility had to be open until five or six, maybe even later, since at this time of the year, the sun didn't start to set until almost seven. That would still give me plenty of time to head over there after work and ask Shawn Zales a few pointed questions.

And hope like hell that he'd actually tell me the truth.

Those last two hours at Levitation Latte dragged like the final class before summer vacation, but at last I was able to lock the doors, help Deanne with wiping down the tables and cleaning out the espresso machine, and then slip out the back. The whole time, I did my best not to show how anxious I was to be on my way, but she must have noticed something, because she said as she was untying her apron, "Hot date with Max this afternoon or something?"

I wrinkled my nose at her. "Not funny."

The smile she'd been wearing stayed fixed in place. "It just seems like you have somewhere you needed to be."

"No," I replied. "I mean, I have to stop at the store on the way home to pick up a couple of things, but that's it."

She still looked a little dubious, but, to my relief, she didn't pursue the matter further. "Well, to be fair, it has felt like an awfully long week, even if it's only Wednesday."

A sentiment I totally agreed with. Okay, it had been my bright idea to open the shop on Sunday so I could do some brain-picking, but I wasn't used to working six days straight and would be very happy when Saturday finally rolled around.

We said goodbye and both got into our cars. Hers was a lot newer than mine, a shiny white Toyota Rav-4 she'd bought only the year before.

Even though I supposed I could have afforded to drive something other than my 2006 Subaru, I was fine with it and planned to keep using the thing until I'd run it into the ground.

After all, I wasn't trying to impress anyone.

Because I'd told Deanne I planned to go to the grocery store, I headed north on 7th Street for a few blocks before doubling back so I could turn onto Cinder Road and drop in at the storage facility Shawn Zales was supposedly managing.

It was the last business located on the street before the land opened up and became populated by ranchettes of three or four acres each, some with horses, a few with goats. The spot where the storage place was located had been a vacant lot for as long as I could remember, and so the business's construction had been the topic of some gossip and speculation until everyone in town realized there wasn't going to be anything terribly interesting built on the empty parcel, only yet another storage facility.

As I pulled into one of the three visitor parking spaces located at the gate, I took a quick look around. The place looked like pretty much every other establishment of its type I'd ever seen—i.e. long rows of low buildings with roll-up doors of various sizes set into the concrete—but this one was clearly newer and shinier than most. There was also what appeared to be an apartment built above the office. If getting to live there was part of Shawn's compensation, the whole setup looked like a pretty good deal.

I got out of my car and did my best to ignore the nervous butterflies fluttering around in my stomach. As much as I'd tried to analyze the situation, there didn't seem to be too many ways of approaching Shawn beyond asking him point-blank if he'd let Evan Bryant into the storage unit the *Perdition Row* crew had been renting. It was an odd enough question that I hadn't figured out how to approach the topic a bit more obliquely.

Well, I'd just have to hope I caught Shawn enough off guard that he'd blurt out the truth.

There was a bell set into the doorframe at the office, and so I pushed it and waited. A minute or so later, Shawn Zales appeared.

He'd always been a big guy, but unlike Evan, he'd gotten thinner since high school, now looking more like someone who went out and shot hoops on the weekend than a man who'd once earned a football scholarship to the state university. But his biceps still appeared pretty chunky as they peeped out from under his loose gray polo shirt emblazoned with the storage facility's logo, and he definitely didn't seem like the sort of person you'd want to tangle with.

Not that I had any intention of getting into a confrontation. No, I just wanted to gather what information I could and then get the heck out of there.

Shawn's light blue eyes narrowed a bit as he caught sight of me standing there. "Skye?" he said, sounding a bit incredulous.

Maybe I should have been grateful that he'd even remembered my name. But since I was here on a mission, I figured I might as well plow forward. "Hi, Shawn," I replied. "How's it going?"

"Fine," he said, his tone now guarded, as though he'd guessed I wasn't there simply to rent a storage unit. If I ever actually got around to clearing out the garage, I might have need of one for the stuff I simply couldn't bear to toss, but that day seemed pretty far off in the future.

Might as well grab the bull by the horns. "Can I ask you something?"

"What?" he replied, now sounding more wary than ever.

"Did you let Evan Bryant into the unit that film crew was renting?"

Shawn crossed his arms and stared at me, expression shifting from caution to shock. A good poker player, he was not.

"How'd you find out about that?"

I supposed I should have been glad I wasn't dealing with a Rhodes scholar here. Otherwise, he might not have blurted out something so obviously incriminating. And his obvious surprise told me that either the police hadn't questioned him at all, or even if they had, they hadn't said anything about Evan because they would have absolutely no reason to believe he was involved.

"I have my ways," I said, doing my best to sound mysterious.

His lip curled. "Still doing that witchy stuff, huh?"

If that was what he wanted to call it, fine. And if Shane's misguided belief that I possessed all sorts of supernatural powers made him more inclined to spill the beans, then I wasn't going to worry about the small subterfuge.

Instead of answering directly, I said, "So, you did let Evan into the unit. How did you keep that little stunt from being recorded?"

Because, even though I didn't have much experience with storage facilities, I'd noticed there was a closed-circuit camera mounted on the wall above the office door, and so I had to believe there were similar cameras located around the facility.

Wouldn't the police have asked Shane to hand over those recordings?

He glanced up at the camera, then said, stony-faced, "CCTV fails sometimes, you know."

In other words, he'd made sure the camera near the particular unit the production crew was renting had failed, or maybe he'd just shut all of them off so there would have been no record off Evan being here at all. And, judging by how uncomfortable Shane now looked, I guessed he was now doubly worried that their maneuverings might have been discovered.

Figuring I'd better plow ahead, I asked, "Did Evan tell you what he wanted in there?"

For a second or two, Shawn paused, his gaze furtively darting around as if to make sure we didn't have an audience, although we were the only two people in the vicinity. Even the street just beyond the storage facility was quiet.

Then he reached up to scratch his blond head and said, obviously doing his best to sound casual, "He said he wanted to play a joke on Max. It was no big deal."

Some joke, shooting the director so he could frame Max for the crime. I didn't mention that, however. It was pretty clear that Shane was in some serious denial, and I didn't want to say anything that might make him clam up. For now, I just wanted to get as much information as I could before making my escape.

"What kind of joke?" I asked.

Shane glanced away from me. Every single line of his body seemed to signal that he wished he was someplace far, far from here. Maybe he'd put two and two together days ago, even if he didn't want to admit to himself that his cooperation with

Evan's "joke" had led to an innocent man's murder.

All right, I wasn't sure if I could classify Perry Lockhart as "innocent," but he definitely shouldn't have gotten dragged into Evan and Raylene's mess.

"I don't know what the joke was," Shane said. "Evan didn't tell me."

No, he probably wouldn't have gone around advertising that he wanted to steal a gun so he could set up Max as the murderer. "You didn't see what he took?"

"Nope." Once again, Shawn ran a hand through his hair, ruffling his already mussed locks. "He was carrying a duffel bag, and so I guessed that whatever he'd taken, it was in there."

Concealing the gun safe, which would have been conspicuous. I wondered how Evan had broken into it, but he probably could have used a lock pick or something. Those portable safes were a clear deterrent to casual crime, but they definitely weren't impenetrable. I realized then that Kyle hadn't said anything about the condition of the gun safe when the police recovered it from the storage unit. However, they'd probably reasoned that Max wouldn't have had the combo and so had done what he needed to in order to break into the safe...especially since he'd played several roles that required the use of a lock pick and therefore might have acquired the actual skill rather than just playing at it.

Before I could say anything in response to his comment, Shawn added, now sounding worried, "I didn't think it was a good idea, but I couldn't really stop him."

"Oh," I retorted as I sent him a skeptical glance, "why not? Did he hold a gun to your head?"

Oops...bad wording.

Shawn shoved his hands in the pockets of his jeans and scowled down at me. "No," he muttered, even as his gaze shifted away toward the street once again. "But his dad owns this storage company. It was Evan who got me the job. I owed him one. It was just for a joke, anyway."

I stared at him in rebuke at that "joke" comment, and he raised guilty eyes to meet mine. "You seriously still think it was just for a joke?" I demanded.

He was too tanned to exactly go pale, but I could tell my question got to him. "No. I mean, I don't know. Look, I didn't have anything to do with any of this!"

Well, except for providing the means of execution, one that would make sure Max looked like the guilty party. But I didn't bother to say any of that. This was all way beyond my pay grade, so I'd let the police chief and the D.A. figure out Shawn Zales' level of culpability.

"He brought it back," Shawn said next, now sounding desperate.

"Of course he did," I said wearily. "Because he wanted the police to find the gun with Max's prints all over it."

Shawn's hands were still shoved in his pockets, but I had feeling they were now clenched into fists, even if I couldn't see them. "What're you going to do?" he asked, his tone almost resigned, as though he'd realized the jig was up and there wasn't much he could do about it.

"What I have to," I said, and took a step backward toward my car, and then another. I wasn't out of range if he decided to lunge for me, but apparently he'd decided he was already in deep enough without adding assault to his list of transgressions, because he only stood there and watched me as I hurried over to my Subaru and got behind the wheel.

I didn't look back as I sped away.

As I headed for home, I wondered what my next step should be. Should I call the police directly with my suspicions, or should I contact Max and let him know what I'd found so he and his attorney could discuss what to do next?

Both options had their merits and their drawbacks. For one thing, I feared if I went to the police right away, they'd want to know why I'd suspected Evan at all. Explaining that I'd found some tea leaves in the shape of a wolf's head in my teacup—and that the leaves had pointed me in the direction of the town's former Lobos football players—would probably get me laughed right out of the station.

On the other hand, if I handed over my information to Max, he might want to take matters into his own hands and deal with Evan directly. Knowing that his erstwhile friend had done his best to frame him for murder might be just the thing to send him charging over to the Ford dealership to hand out some western-style justice.

My head hurt.

Well, I was almost home. I could brew myself some tea...and studiously avoid looking at the leaves...and then weigh the pros and cons of what I should do with the information I'd just gotten from Shawn Zales.

With the matter decided, I kept heading south on 12th Street, and then turned onto my street and into my driveway. A quick look around told me the paparazzo's silver SUV wasn't anywhere in evidence, so it looked as though he really had been sent packing.

Good. I went up the back stairs and into the kitchen. The first order of business was getting the kettle filled and the gas going on the stove. Something friendly and soothing to drink, like peppermint. Its clean, fresh aroma might be just the thing to help clear my head and allow me to figure out what I should do next.

Since the kettle hadn't been full, it didn't take long for the water to get hot enough to brew some tea. Once it was ready, I took my mug—a nicely glazed stoneware piece painted with cheerful red and yellow flowers—into the living room, along with my cell phone. That way, if I decided to call Max, I wouldn't have to go back into the kitchen to retrieve it.

A few sips of tea made me feel better almost immediately, although I still felt edgy, not quite ready to sit down. Even so, I thought this was definitely the best thing for me to have done.

Almost without thinking, I reached for my phone. It just seemed wisest to get in contact with Max first and tell him what I knew, and then he could make the decision as to whether we should pass the information along to his attorney or go straight to the police.

To my relief, he picked up right away. "Hey, Skye," he said. "What's up?"

"I think I figured it out," I told him, and then launched into a full explanation about the tea leaves and the connection between Evan and Shawn Zales, and the stolen gun.

"'Evan'?" Max repeated, sounding both angry and mystified. "Why the hell would Evan Bryant want to do something like this to me?"

"Because he was jealous," I said at once. I thought then of that almost-nightmare where I'd bumped into Raylene in the supermarket. In the dream, she'd said, "*He* loves me," and at the time, I'd thought she was talking about Max.

But she wasn't. No, she'd been talking about her husband, the man who must have been consumed with murderous rage when he found out she'd been carrying a torch for her ex all these years.

Okay, that was all pure speculation on my part. But my prickly sixth sense or instinct or whatever you wanted to call it was telling me that was exactly what had happened. Somehow, Evan must have found the letters Raylene had gotten from Max telling her why they'd never be a couple again—and possibly even found a copy of the restraining order —and then when he realized Max was coming to Las Vegas to shoot a movie, he'd finally be able to enact his revenge.

Or I could be completely off base. I'd let the police and the lawyers dig up all the hows and whys. For the moment, the most important thing was to let them know who the real guilty party was here.

"Oh," Max said flatly, and then, "Oh, shit. Of course. He was pissed about Raylene."

"Exactly," I replied. "So, do you want to talk to your lawyer first, or—"

"Put down the phone."

Startled, I glanced over toward the short hall that led to the kitchen. Standing there, nearly filling the space with his bulk, was Evan Bryant.

CHAPTER 16

Deus ex Max

Evan was holding an ugly, snub-nosed pistol and had it pointed straight at me. As I stared back at him in consternation, he said again, the words coming out slowly, like he was talking to someone hard of hearing, "Put. Down. The. Phone."

I swallowed and set the phone down on the coffee table...but I didn't end the call. No, I needed Max to hear this.

Speaking a little more loudly than I normally would, I said, "Evan, how did you get in my house? What's with the gun?"

That sneering little smirk was back on his lips. "You shouldn't be so careless, Skye. I mean, I know this is a pretty safe neighborhood, but you should really lock your back door."

In an echo of Max's words from a few minutes

earlier, *Oh, shit* passed through my mind. There I'd been, hurrying into the house, intent on making myself some tea, and I'd completely forgotten to turn around and engage the deadbolt on the kitchen door. It wasn't the first time I'd made that mistake.

I just had to hope it wouldn't be my last.

"Oops," I said, and summoned a goofy little grin I doubted would have fooled anyone, let alone the man who loomed in front of me, that ugly gun still pointed directly at my heart...the same place where he'd shot Perry. But because I had no idea how else to handle the situation—I'd never had anyone aim a gun at me before—I just kept playing dumb. "But seriously, Evan, what're you doing with that gun?"

His eyes narrowed for a second, and then he glanced from me to the phone where it sat on the coffee table. Without saying anything, he came closer, looked down at it...and an ugly scowl twisted his features before he picked it up and slammed it against the wall.

The phone shattered into roughly a thousand pieces, bits of metal and plastic flying everywhere, tinkling against the hardwood floor. It was a strangely delicate sound, not what I would have associated with such an act of violence.

Irrelevantly, I wondered whether the extended

warranty would cover situations like this. I'd have to call Apple and find out.

Assuming I survived the next few minutes, that is.

Without answering me directly, Evan said, "You just couldn't leave it alone, could you? No, you had to stick your big nose in where it didn't belong."

It took a supreme effort of will to keep myself from reaching up to give my nose a self-conscious rub. Yes, I'd grown into it over the years, and now actually liked my schnozz on most days, but I still didn't like being reminded of the way Evan and his friends—including Raylene—used to tease me, calling me "honker" and "walrus" and a choice selection of even less polite phrases.

"I was just trying to help Max," I replied. "For some reason, I'm not a big fan of people who try to frame my best friend for murder."

"'Best friend'?" Evan repeated in scoffing tones. "I bet you haven't even talked to the guy in years."

That comment showed how much he knew, considering I'd just been speaking with Max when Evan showed up and started waving his gun around.

"Hmm," I said, and pushed a skeptical finger against my chin. "Smells like someone's jealous."

"Of you?" Evan shot back, another ugly sneer

pulling at his mouth. The gun hadn't wavered during this entire exchange, but at least he seemed distracted enough to have refrained from pulling the trigger.

Good. Keeping him occupied seemed to be the only way to prolong my life, if only for a few more minutes. I kept hoping I'd soon hear the wail of a police siren, letting me know that Max had figured out what was going on and had called the cops.

Whether any of Las Vegas's finest were really up to the task of taking down an armed and desperate man was a topic for an entirely different debate. In the meantime, though, I knew I had to hope for the best.

And do my best to prevent the worst.

"Of course not of *me*," I said, now planting my hands on my hips. For the first time, the gun in Evan's grip wavered just the slightest bit, but then he seemed to realize I wasn't trying to make a sudden run for it, was only shifting my stance slightly. "Of *Max*. It must have really burned you to find out Raylene was still pining for him after all these years...and all those kids."

Evan's muddy hazel eyes narrowed. "Shut up."

That less than scintillating rejoinder told me I'd struck a nerve. The trick would be to keep him talking without provoking him into actually pulling the trigger. On the wall behind me, my grandmother's antique clock ticked serenely away, telling me that time was indeed passing.

Where the hell were the cops?

"But then you found out Max was coming to Las Vegas, and you decided to take revenge, right?" I went on doggedly. At this point, I knew I just had to keep going. Besides, I had to admit that I really wanted to know whether my theory regarding Evan's motive for murdering Perry Lockhart was correct. "Only it wouldn't be good enough to just shoot him, would it? No, you thought it would be better to frame Max for murder, and then sit by and watch while he lost everything he worked so hard for. And when you realized that your friend Shawn could give you access to the actual weapon Max had been using on set, it seemed like the perfect setup."

I paused there and sent Evan a searching look. For a guy supposedly in control of the situation, he wasn't looking too good—a sheen of sweat covered his forehead up to his already receding hairline, and his face looked blotchy and pale under its late-summer tan.

"Does Raylene know about all this?" I asked when it seemed he hadn't been able to summon the words for an adequate rebuttal to my remarks. "Did she also want a little revenge for being a woman scorned?"

"No," Evan snapped. He now looked even angrier, eyes narrow and mouth tight, and a cold little thrill of fear went through me.

Had I pushed him too far?

But then he seemed to regain some control, because he said, "Raylene doesn't know anything. I mean, she knows I found those letters from Max, but she tried to tell me she was just going through a bad patch and that it didn't amount to anything."

Well, nothing beyond Max being so concerned about her unwanted attention that he'd had to get a restraining order against the woman. But because Evan hadn't mentioned anything about that particular facet of the situation, I thought it better to keep my mouth shut on the topic.

"Then that should have been the end of it, shouldn't it?" I said. "I mean, it sounds like the sort of thing where it would have been better to go to marriage counseling rather than resort to murder."

One side of Evan's mouth lifted in what looked almost like a snarl. For just a second, he actually resembled his college mascot, with his bared teeth and that feral, frightening gleam in his eyes.

"You don't know what you're talking about," he said, and this time the gun moved for real, shifting from an imaginary target on my chest to one that felt as though it was directly between my eyes. Cold sweat dripped down my back, icy from the air conditioning that blew through the vent above me. "And now I have to make sure you'll never use that big mouth to talk about anything again."

His finger tightened on the trigger, and my heart began to pound so hard, I thought for sure Evan could hear it all the way across the room.

"What about Shawn?" I asked, knowing how desperate I sounded and not caring too much. "He knows what you've done. You think killing me is going to make all this go away?"

"Shawn will keep his mouth shut," Evan responded. "He doesn't want to lose his job and the place he's been living." Now he sounded almost relaxed, as though he figured he could stop worrying now that he knew he was going to shoot me in the next second or two.

"But the police—"

"The police don't know a damn thing," he broke in. "And even if they do manage to put two and two together, my father will make it all go away."

Evan's finger moved on the trigger, and I tensed, wondering how much it hurt to get shot in the head, whether I'd know I was dead or whether it would just be *blam!* and darkness, or maybe pearly gates and angels singing if I were really lucky.

None of those things happened, though, because even as I braced myself and waited for a bullet to emerge from the pistol's barrel, Max broke into the room and barreled right into Evan, catching him from behind and knocking him to the floor. The gun fell from Evan's hand and skittered across the polished oak boards. He scrabbled for it, cursing, and I broke free from my shocked paralysis, stumbled over to the spot where it had fallen, and kicked it safely out of the way. Maybe some people would have picked it up, but because I'd never shot a gun in my life, I thought it would be better for everyone concerned if the damn thing was inaccessible under the couch.

Evan let out a pained "oof!" as Max dug his knee into the small of his former friend's back, then grabbed both of his hands and yanked them behind him, lashing his wrists and then his ankles with a couple of bright yellow zip ties. That task accomplished, he staggered to his feet and looked over at me, even as Evan began thrashing around on the floor like a beached whale, flinging one curse after another at his rival as he tried to free himself.

"You okay?" Max asked as he brushed off his jeans, which looked as though they'd survived the scuffle relatively unscathed.

"I'm fine," I said after a quick pause to make sure I really was all right. Keyed up and shaky, thanks to the adrenaline still surging through my veins, but since Evan had never actually laid a hand on me, physically I was doing better than expected. "Where'd you get the zip ties?"

"From Lou," Max replied. Off in the distance, sirens wailed, coming closer. He went to the front window and peered out. "Actually, he drove me over here. Said it would be better for him to get the speeding ticket if the cops tried to pull us over."

On shaky legs, I closed up the distance between us so I could stand next to him, and then looked out the window as well. Sure enough, there was Max's rented Bronco parked right in front of the house. He made a thumbs-up signal, apparently to let Lou know that everything was okay, although I couldn't see the security guard from where I stood.

"That was quite the maneuver you pulled," I remarked, and looked back at where Evan was still straining—with absolutely no luck—against his plastic bonds.

Max shrugged. "Hey, you don't work on all those action movies without picking up a few tricks."

About all I could do was let out a weak chuckle.

"I'm just glad you're okay," he went on. "When I heard Evan's voice on the phone, I knew I had to get over here right away."

And before I could say anything, Max reached over and pulled me into a quick, fierce hug. This was the first time I was able to feel those impressive muscles for myself, and I was so shocked that I just stood there in the circle of his arms for a moment before he let go again. While there hadn't been anything particularly romantic about the embrace,

I was still a little gobsmacked that he'd done such a thing at all. After he let go, I immediately returned my attention to the window, since I knew I didn't want him to see what might have been revealed in my expression right then.

The sirens got closer, and I watched as a couple of squad cars pulled up to the curb. Four officers got out of those cars, guns drawn, including Kyle.

"Do you want to tell them, or should I?" Max said, and I looked up at him.

"Tell them what?"

He sent me one of those dazzling grins, a smile I had no doubt I would see up on the big screen once again in the not-too-distant future.

"That we already caught the bad guy."

The story was definitely a ten-day wonder around Las Vegas, and occupied a good chunk of time on even the national news until the sensation about Max Sullivan being unsuccessfully framed for murder died down and the media found a different scandal to latch on to. Evan vigorously denied any wrongdoing, of course, but since the gun I'd kicked under the sofa had his prints on it and no one else's, he was obviously guilty of aggravated assault if nothing else.

But then Shawn Zales came forward and spilled

the whole story to Chief DeVargas, and even Raylene—much to my surprise—admitted how she had tried writing Max a bunch of times several years earlier and that Evan had pretty much lost his mind over it. Plus, there was the record of my conversation with him, subpoenaed from the phone company, when he came over to shoot me dead. True, we hadn't gotten very far before he picked up my poor iPhone and flung it into the wall, but because the little convo ended with me asking him why he had a gun, even that snippet was pretty incriminating.

So, he got to cool his heels in the San Miguel County lockup until he could be formally arraigned, whereupon the judge deemed him a risk to the entire community and commanded that he stay in jail until his court date...which, ironically, was the same day Max would have had to defend himself against those trumped-up murder charges.

All the charges had been dropped, obviously, but Max hadn't gone back to L.A. No, he'd hung around on his rented ranch, saying that since he'd already planned to be there until the end of the month anyway, he might as well stay for the duration and allow the whole scandal to die down a bit.

Which I could completely understand. If I were in his position, I wouldn't have wanted to go back to L.A. and deal with paparazzi camped out waiting for me to emerge from Spago, or wherever it was that celebrities went out to eat these days. I had to admit I wasn't too up on that sort of thing.

And Levitation Latte had been even busier than usual these past few weeks, mostly because people wanted to come in and hear the story straight from the horse's mouth, so to speak. I only had one side of it, but that seemed to be good enough for them. After all, nothing this exciting had ever happened in the history of Las Vegas—or at least, not since its early Wild West days.

"It's actually almost as good as having a movie filmed here, don't you think?" Deanne asked me on a Friday afternoon near the end of the month, just as I was wearily closing the doors to the shop and making sure they were locked. The hordes had picked us clean that day, so at least I didn't have to worry about putting away any surplus muffins or croissants.

"Well, except for the part about Evan Bryant almost blowing my head off," I responded. I moved over to one of the tables and began to wipe it down, marveling a bit at the assortment of crumbs a group of high school students had left behind as they'd shared my last two apple spice muffins.

Deanne planted a hand on her hip. "I thought you said Max knocked the gun out of his hand before he could do anything."

A little shudder moved over me as I recalled that tense, somehow endless moment. "He did," I replied, "but I heard that trigger click. It was still way too close."

Close enough that I still had nightmares of staring down the barrel of that gun, of it seeming to get bigger and bigger until it turned into a yawning cavern that threatened to swallow me whole. Each time, I awoke with my breath coming in pants and my body slick with cold sweat, even as I reassured myself that Evan was safely in jail and couldn't possibly be coming for me. The only real upside was that I could tell these weren't true dreams, just my subconscious mind messing with me as it tried to work its way through the trauma.

Deanne's expression sobered, and she didn't try to argue with me. After all, I'd been there, and she hadn't. Voice quiet but firm, she said, "He's going away for a long, long time."

I didn't have to read the leaves to sense the truth of that statement. His father had hired him a high-priced criminal defense attorney from Albuquerque, and yet I knew in my bones that I'd never have to worry about Evan Bryant again.

Max had texted me earlier in the day asking if I could come by after work, and of course I'd said yes. To tell the truth, we hadn't seen a lot of each other since the fateful moment when he'd come to my rescue. Oh, he'd dropped by the coffee shop once, and his parents had invited me over for dinner a few nights afterward to thank me for proving their son's innocence, but otherwise, he'd seemed pretty occupied. He'd done a lot of interviews, of course, and it sounded as though the film in January was back on. All the same, I'd gotten the feeling he just wanted to hole up at the ranch until all this blew over.

Again, completely understandable.

Because we hadn't agreed on a set time for my arrival, I made a quick detour to the house so I could change into a new pair of jeans, ones that didn't have smudges of flour on them, and a nicer top than the black T-shirt I'd worn to work, and also to fuss with my hair a bit and freshen my makeup. Maybe all this primping was entirely unnecessary, and yet I still felt better after doing it. In my mind, something had changed between Max and me that horrible day when Evan broke into the house. He'd come charging to my rescue, had held me afterward, obviously relieved I was all right. Those might have been the actions of a friend and nothing more, but....

I told myself not to get my hopes up, that if he was really so interested in being something more than good friends, he'd had all this time to reach out and talk. Then again, he'd just been through a lot as well. Anyone who knew him would probably say Max was the kind of guy who generally went charging headlong into a situation without stopping to think first, but it was possible he'd decided he needed to slow himself down in this particular case.

And so on, and so on, inventing possibilities and then rejecting them before moving on to a brand-new scenario. My brain could really be a pain in the butt when it came to Max Sullivan.

Once again, Lou was watching the gate as I drove up. This time, he waved me through with a smile, and I smiled back. Thanks to him, he'd gotten Max to my house on that terrible afternoon in pretty much record time. If they'd been even a minute later....

But they hadn't been. Lou was apparently a former stunt driver, and so he'd made that black Bronco fly.

I parked in front of the garage and got out of my Subaru, then headed to the front door. No sign of Max, and so I rang the doorbell and waited.

A minute later, he opened the door and smiled down at me. It seemed pretty obvious that he must have been spending some of the past few weeks hanging out in the pool and relaxing, because he looked tanned and utterly rested, like a guy who'd just gotten back from an extended vacation in the Bahamas.

"Hey, Skye," he said. "Come on in."

All the windows were open, letting a fresh breeze move through the house. In a few more weeks, it might not be warm enough for that sort of thing, but I could see why he'd want to enjoy it in the meantime.

"I thought we'd sit on the patio," he went on as I followed him to the kitchen. "What do you want to drink? Wine? Beer? A margarita?"

Part of me could have really gone for a margarita right then, but I spied an open beer bottle on the counter and realized I didn't want to make Max go to that much work when it was clear he'd already decided on his poison of choice for the afternoon.

"A glass of wine would be great," I told him. "Something white, if you've got it."

"Coming right up."

He went to the fridge and brought out a bottle of pinot grigio, one that had obviously been opened already, since it had one of those little rubber stoppers in it to keep the wine from oxidizing. After pouring me a glass, he gestured toward the patio.

"Let's go."

A sensation of *déjà vu* swept over me as I settled myself on the love seat and Max sat down on the couch immediately to my right. Just like the last time we'd gathered here, the wind was brisk but warm, bringing with it a scent of dry grass and juniper that always made me think of home.

"Sorry I've made myself scarce these past couple of weeks," he said as I took my first sip of pinot grigio. "There's just been a lot going on."

"You don't need to apologize," I replied, then sent Max a sly smile. "I know you were doing interviews all over the place."

His answering smile was a bit crooked, as though he'd started to grimace and self-corrected. "All part of the job, unfortunately. But at least the hubbub has mostly died down now. I'm thinking of sending Kim Kardashian a fruit basket—she and her new boyfriend did a good job of getting the monkeys off my back."

About all I could do was shake my head. That did seem to be standard operating procedure when it came to celebrity journalists...they were always chasing after the new and shiny thing.

"And Margaret, my agent, says her phone won't stop ringing," he went on. "I guess proving myself as a real-life action hero has a bunch of directors wanting to cast me in their latest franchise."

"No more art films?" I teased, even as I did my best to ignore the stab of disappointment that went through me at his words. Max had already been in huge demand, and if he was getting all this additional interest, I had to believe his calendar would be full for the next two years...or more.

"I doubt it," he said, still smiling. "The thing is, I realized something, coming back here."

"You did?" The disappointment fled, replaced by a hope I wasn't sure I wanted to acknowledge.

Had he asked me out to the ranch so he could reveal his true feelings for me?

My fingers tightened on the stem of the wine glass I held, but I didn't say anything else, only waited, even as my heart started pounding a mile a minute in my chest.

Max looked away from me, at the gorgeous vista beyond the garden—the majestic contours of the Sangre de Cristo mountains' eastern slopes, now brushed with sunlit gold as the day wore to its close, the lush green of the cottonwoods in the creek that wound its way through the property.

"I realized how much I missed this place," he said at length. "Las Vegas, I mean. It's my hometown, and I sort of pushed it out of my mind, just because of everything else that was going on in my life. But being here—being away from L.A. and all the craziness—made me think I needed to have this back."

"Oh?" I managed. Disappointment had already started to trickle back in, even as I tried to tell myself that I was part of Las Vegas, part of the life he'd left behind when he'd become Max Sullivan, movie star. Just because he'd mentioned only his hometown and not me didn't necessarily mean anything.

Yeah, right.

Another pause, and then he shifted so his eyes met mine. In them, I saw a sort of repressed excitement...and possibly something else, a warmth that hadn't been there a few minutes earlier.

Or maybe I was just imagining things because I really, really needed to right then.

"And that's why I bought the ranch," he concluded.

I stared back at him, not sure how I should respond to that confounding statement. "I didn't know it was for sale," I said after a pause, my tone flat.

His smile didn't waver. "Not formally...but you know what they say about offers you can't refuse."

Yes, I did. And Max had so much money that I doubted the owners of the ranch would have done much beyond signing on the dotted line.

"So...you're going to live in Las Vegas?" I asked next. My voice sounded almost normal, a fact for which I was extremely grateful. I'd managed to hide my feelings all these years, and I was going to continue to do so now.

Even if it killed me.

"Well, as much as I can," he replied. "I mean, I'll

be shooting two to three movies a year, so I'll have to be away a lot. But I'll come back as often as I can." An enthusiastic light shone in his bright blue eyes, and he finally raised his bottle of beer to his lips and took a large swallow. "It's going to be a blast!"

"A blast," I echoed weakly, and drank some of my wine, my head spinning as I began to consider all the ramifications of this revelation.

Max Sullivan's troubles might have been over... but it looked as though mine were just beginning.

Skye's adventures continue in *Muffins After Magic,* releasing in October 2022.

Also by Christine Pope

LATTES AND LEVITATION

(Cozy mystery/Paranormal romance)

Caffeine Before Curses

Muffins After Magic

Pastries and Prophecies (March 2023)

UNEXPECTED MAGIC

(Urban fantasy/Paranormal romance)

Found Objects

Finders, Keepers

Lost and Found

Finding Destiny (January 2023)

HEDGEWITCH FOR HIRE

(Mystery/Paranormal romance)

Grave Mistake

Social Medium

Household Demons

Perpetual Potion

Jingle Spells

Wandering Monsters

Uninvited Ghosts

Prophet Motive (November 2022)

THE WITCHES OF WHEELER PARK*

(Paranormal romance)

Storm Born

Thunder Road

Winds of Change

Mind Games

A Wheeler Park Christmas

Blood Ties

Healing Hands

Wishful Thinking

Smoke and Mirrors

MISS PRIMM'S ACADEMY FOR WAYWARD WITCHES*

(Fantasy/Academy Romance)

Misspelled

Dispelled

Expelled

PROJECT DEMON HUNTERS*

(Paranormal Romance)

Unquiet Souls

Unbound Spirits

Unholy Ground

Unseen Voices

Unmarked Graves

Unbroken Vows

THE DEVIL YOU KNOW*

(Paranormal Romance)

Sympathy for the Devil

Charmed, I'm Sure

A Wing and a Prayer

Wish Upon a Star

THE WITCHES OF CANYON ROAD*

(Paranormal Romance)

Hidden Gifts

Darker Paths

Mysterious Ways

A Canyon Road Christmas

Demon Born

An Ill Wind

Higher Ground

Haunted Hearts

THE WITCHES OF CLEOPATRA HILL*

(Paranormal Romance)

Darkangel

Darknight

Darkmoon

Sympathetic Magic

Protector

Spellbound

A Cleopatra Hill Christmas

Impractical Magic

Strange Magic

THE WATCHERS TRILOGY*

(Paranormal Romance)

Falling Dark

Dead of Night

Rising Dawn

THE SEDONA FILES*

(Paranormal Romance)

Bad Vibrations

Desert Hearts

Angel Fire

Star Crossed

Falling Angels

Enemy Mine

TALES OF THE LATTER KINGDOMS*

(Fantasy Romance)

All Fall Down

Dragon Rose

Binding Spell

Ashes of Roses

One Thousand Nights

Threads of Gold

The Wolf of Harrow Hall

Moon Dance

The Song of the Thrush

THE GAIAN CONSORTIUM SERIES*

(Science Fiction Romance)

Beast (free prequel novella)

Blood Will Tell

Breath of Life

The Gaia Gambit

The Mandala Maneuver

The Titan Trap

The Zhore Deception

The Refugee Ruse

STANDALONE TITLES

Hearts on Fire

Taking Dictation

Golden Heart

Night Music: A Modern Reimagining of The Phantom of the Opera

Ghost Dance: A Sequel to Gaston Leroux's The Phantom of the Opera

Flight Before Christmas

* Indicates a completed series

About the Author

USA Today bestselling author Christine Pope has been writing stories ever since she commandeered her family's Smith-Corona typewriter back in grade school. Her work includes paranormal romance, fantasy romance, and science fiction/space opera romance. She makes her home in New Mexico.

Don't miss out on any of Christine's new releases —sign up for her newsletter today!

Christine Pope on the Web:
www.christinepope.com